Algernon Gissing

The Scholar of Bygate

A tale. Vol. 3

Algernon Gissing

The Scholar of Bygate
A tale. Vol. 3

ISBN/EAN: 9783337344184

Printed in Europe, USA, Canada, Australia, Japan

Cover: Foto ©Andreas Hilbeck / pixelio.de

More available books at **www.hansebooks.com**

The
Scholar of Bygate

A Tale

BY

ALGERNON GISSING

Author of " A Moorland Idyl," &c.

IN THREE VOLUMES

VOL. III.

LONDON
HUTCHINSON & CO.
34 PATERNOSTER ROW, E.C.
1897

CONTENTS OF THIRD VOLUME.

THE SCHOLAR OF BYGATE

CHAPTER I.

IN THE BALANCE.

As Adelina walked into the room, her husband turned round to greet her, and with a brighter face than she had expected, came forward to fold her in his arms. He held her face upwards with one hand at her chin, as he playfully planted one kiss after another on her plump, little, rosy lips, which from mere coquettish instinct she gathered up for the purpose. But she was glad when he released her, and Sibbald felt perfectly aware of the fact as he did so.

She did not know why his kisses should burn her so, or why she should shrink so vehemently from his caresses. All her face was hot and crimson as she drew away towards the window, and she could only stammer, "I got your letter."

"Yes, I ought to have sent you word before, but I never thought of being away for the night. I had to go over to Bygate before the sale, and as—"

She turned round abruptly to face him.

"Sale! Is the house going to be sold?" exclaimed she.

"Yes, everything is to be sold," he replied, calmly sustaining her gaze.

"But what for? Is your father bankrupt?"

"No, he is not bankrupt," began Sibbald with knitted brows and a fiery tone, which, however, he managed to soften. "No, he is only coming to live in the town. I suppose he is tired of country life, like we are."

"But aren't you sorry? I thought you were so fond of the place. You once told me that you would never live anywhere else."

" I once thought I never should. Now I don't much mind where I live—so long as I can make you happy, dearest," he added as a conscious after-thought.

" It is awfully good of you, Sib. But Bygate to be sold! What a strange thing! And you take it as a matter of course. I don't understand it."

" Then I am lying to you if I seem to take it as a matter of course, Lina," ejaculated Crozier, the colour in his face heightening. " It is like tearing out my heart by the roots, but I can do nothing to stop it—nothing at all."

" I suppose it's through me that he is selling it," said Lina with a sudden flash of intuition, and fixing her eyes upon him with almost a savage glare in them. " That'll be it, I'm certain. He's going to cut you off because you married me. Isn't that it, Sib? I insist upon you telling me."

She advanced imperiously towards him.

"It is through your father as much as you. If he—"

"How you hate us both! . . . No wonder you have changed towards me! No wonder you leave me whole days and nights alone. I wonder you ever came back to me at all."

Lina was determined to make use of the pitch she had worked herself up to before meeting him.

"What *are* you talking about, dear? Don't get so excited about it. You must think me a poor, miserable scoundrel if you can suppose that I can attribute this to you. What if it was solely on account of my marrying you; do you think I should hate you for it? Do you think I should put one particle of the blame upon you? You cannot think so badly of me as that already, Lina. The blame is wholly and solely my own. If I seemed changed towards you, it is only because I have been so harassed lately."

"But you *are* changed, and you do hate me," said she. "You would never go out enjoying yourself at nights alone if you were not sick of me. I'm sure you wouldn't. Nobody could."

As the tears came, Adelina ran out of the room and upstairs to take her things off. Sibbald stood contemplative. This was scarcely the propitious beginning he had looked for, and upon which he had so resolutely set his mind. It only showed him what amount of resolution would be required of him, and he felt depressed and disconcerted. In a minute or two the servant came in to lay their mid-day dinner, and when it was ready, as Lina did not come down, he went up to fetch her.

He found her on the bed passionately weeping, and no efforts of his could pacify her. After trying every tender means that occurred to him, he gave it up, and walked to and fro at the foot of the bedstead, with his hands linked nervously behind him.

After a time Lina calmed herself, and got up, sulky and speechless. An attempted caress from Sibbald was repelled, and she made no answer to his words. So he went downstairs again and began his meal. Halfway through it she appeared, but declined to take a place at the table. She didn't want anything, so she flung herself in an armchair. Her husband finished in silence.

When the table was cleared and they were alone again, Crozier determined to resume the discussion, in the hope of reaching a more satisfactory issue. After the prolonged silence, it was not easy to begin again, but it must be done, so in rather a stiff way he said :

" You are mistaken if you think I go out enjoying myself, Lina. Enjoyment is not much in my calculations at present."

"Not in my company, I know," was the sulky retort, for the suspicion of sympathy which the revelation of his affairs had awakened was now gone.

" You think then that I am different when I am away from you ? "

" I know you are."

The persistently hostile tone which she seemed determined to assume took Sibbald by surprise, for, strained though *he* had felt the relationship, they had parted upon ostensibly affectionate terms. This new development added to his perplexity.

" I wish you would tell me your reason for thinking so."

"People don't go to the Tyne Theatre to be miserable, not even when they go alone."

Sibbald's eyes rested upon her in calm surprise. Hers were lowered whilst her fingers plucked some fancy work on her frock.

"What do you mean, Lina? Have I ever been to the Tyne Theatre do you suppose ? "

" I know you have."

" I should be glad to know of your authority, for it is certainly more than I know myself."

She raised her eyes to him suddenly as though to confuse him in his dissimulation ; but hers were the first to fall,

" You were there a couple of nights ago."

" My darling lassie, you are under some strange mistake. I have never set foot in the Tyne Theatre in my life."

" It's a lie," cried she. " I know you were there." And she started up from her seat in a theatrical manner.

" Then I'll say no more," said Sibbald with cold dignity, smothering his indignation under his constitutional pride. In a few minutes he went out.

Strive as he would, Sibbald could not restore a footing of intimate affection with Lina. She took no trouble to disguise the suspicion which she harboured, or pretended to harbour, against him, and for the days that followed his stock of virtuous patience was put very severely to the test. Any open rupture he simply refused to allow, by the expedient of always withdrawing from a disagreement. In this way, frequently, Lina's ill-humour was foiled, and she would give vent to her feelings in a passionate flood of tears.

The fact was that that one evening of Sibbald's absence had wrought a subtle effect upon Lina. It had shattered her continuity of feeling for her husband, by interposing a wholly inconsistent inclination. In a nature so flimsy and volatile, a breach of the kind was not easily to be mended. All the past could be in an instant extinguished— utterly annihilated, as though it had never been. Deeper natures, even under a change, are permanently modified by past associations,—not so Adelina.

For an instant she was in doubt about that Friday's engagement; not at all about her own determination to keep it, but as to whether she should mention it to Sibbald. It lasted only for an instant, and she decided for wholly independent action. He never told her where he was going, so why she him? He dissembled—nay, lied, she did not hesitate to believe—so why not she? So she went.

Mr. Robson had facetiously hinted at her bringing her husband with her, but Lina was not content to risk the day's enjoyment by mentioning it to him. He *might* just take it into his head to accompany her, and in a vague kind of way she admitted to herself that in that case she would rather stay at home. As it was, going alone, and the elements favouring the enterprise, she had a day of delirious excitement. For that one day she resolved to forget her bonds, and to enter into the humours of the situation as if the last few months of her life had never been. It was delightful to find what power remained with her. She soon found that over Mr. Robson she could exercise unlimited dominion, and, naturally, she did exercise it. The exigencies of the occasion threw them much together, and nothing could have been more agreeable to them.

So exhilarated was she by the enterprise that, when she got home about nine o'clock at night, she had some vivacity still left for her husband. It was not of the kind which now fascinated Sibbald, but it was at least preferable to her petulant temper, so he deliberately made himself cheerful.

"You got my note, Sib?" She had arranged that he should receive one about mid-day, as if the expedition had been improvised. "Wasn't it good of Leila? Oh, I've had a lovely day. Quite a family party of us. In the afternoon we came on to Dilston, and had such fun in the woods."

"I am glad you have enjoyed it so much, darling."

"I can't tell you how much I've enjoyed it," continued she, fluttering to and fro about the room. "That glen where— Oh, have they sent this *here* ?" she suddenly cried, as her eyes rested on a parcel on the sofa, from which the great white printed label of a prominent millinery firm glared at her.

"The stupid—" But she stopped, and tried, not very successfully, to hide her vexation.

"Yes, they tell me it came this afternoon," said Sibbald calmly. "Isn't it for you?"

"Yes, it's for me, but—but of course it doesn't matter."

And resolving to brave it out, she took her scissors and snipped the string there and then. After the rustling of the paper, she rather too defiantly held up a very fascinating blouse for her husband's admiration. He had had some time to tutor himself previously, so he smiled as benignly as she could, wish.

"There! even you like it! Isn't it lovely? I knew you wouldn't be able to resist it, and I knew if you had been there you would have given it me. Of course I should have spoken to you about it, only I was—I was *so* afraid that it might have gone by to-morrow."

In a fit of almost hysterical abandonment at his

unexpected kindness, Adelina swept across the room,
and smothered him in a fragrant and vehement
embrace. There was nothing outwardly to display
Sibbald's shudder under the scented ordeal, and in
the contact he himself succeeded in smothering that
and returning the tenderness with something of his
old fervour towards the ideal woman in her. Some
minutes later they were talking in a more composed
manner.

"Well, Bygate has been sold to-day," said Sibbald,
when a quiet interval had given him the opportunity.

"Oh, really! I had forgotten about that. Did it
sell well? Who bought it?"

" As I expected. Lord Braiddale bought it all for
three thousand pounds; a very good price, I am told.
But, of course, you understand, Lina, that we shall
never see a farthing of that. It is as well to bear it
in mind. I saw Mr. Elliott, the agent who bought it,
and he told me that his lordship was in the town, so
I went to see him."

"Lor', Sib!" Visions, perhaps, of an introduction to a real lordship staggering Adelina for an instant.

"He was remarkably kind to me."

"How good of his lordship."

"I made no secret of my feelings about it, and he fully understood me. That man is fit to be a lord, which is saying a good deal nowadays," exclaimed Crozier, waxing ardent at the thought of his interview. "He suggested that I should become tenant of the place, but I couldn't stand that—"

"No, no, of course not."

"So he said plainly that he should consider himself a steward on my behalf, and if, at any time, I wished to repurchase the place, it should be mine at the sum which he had paid for it."

"Beautiful! . . . Well, that *is* nice!"

"But that is not all. I told him my difficulties about employment, and he at once said that he thought he could almost certainly get me some little place in a bank, if that would do, and I needn't tell you that I accepted his offer."

Lina did not speak immediately. She had been suddenly troubled by the wonder whether Mr. Robson knew a lord, or whether one would treat him with so much consideration.

" That is satisfactory, isn't it ? "

" Oh, very, very. Really delightful."

But that was only a gleam in the generally overcast sky of their existence ; it was impulsive, and it passed. In the common daylight, Adelina found her situation but little more to her taste. Her husband was markedly more attentive to her, showed a deliberate desire to please her, to minister to her pleasure, but in too sober a way to gain altogether the end he wished. She missed the careless irresponsible submission to her whims which had characterised their earlier intercourse. She felt an uneasy suspicion that he was trying to teach her, to lead her into the pleasures that satisfied him. This was by no means her notion of pleasure. The jocular pleasantries of Mr. Charles Robson, for instance, continued very much more to her taste. Moreover, she did not fully trust him.

Adelina's instinctive construction of things was, of course, uncommonly accurate, with the exception of the last particular. Sibbald *was* bending the whole of his efforts to this high task of imparting to his wife some measure of a cultured imagination, and lay under no delusion as to the magnitude of the undertaking. Naturally hot-tempered and impulsive himself, he often was sorely urged to fling off the thankless endeavour, and leave her to her own frivolous devices, but something ever came to brace him to his post again. Within a week Sibbald got a note from the manager of one of the principal banks, which he answered in person. It resulted in a subordinate engagement.

Had anybody suggested to Crozier that Adelina

would get into compromising mischief he would have knocked that body down. When, therefore, he came to be employed all day, his only concern was for her entertainment, and the risk of milliners' bills. Upon this latter point he spoke frankly, and she faithfully promised to attend to his injunctions. With regard to her amusements he soon found that the matter was beyond his control. Devoted to books himself, from boyhood upwards, he tried to exercise some direction over her reading, but in this also he was powerless. She would not confess that she never read a word of the books that he left her, but he soon knew that it was so. She preferred to draw out books for herself or take them on the recommendation of Miss Leila Featherstone. It was a strange idea to Lina that reading should be made a toil, and no persuasion would have induced her to believe that books *he* advised were read by any soul for recreation. So Sibbald knew that day by day they were only drifting further apart, and the knowledge was a source of genuine torment to him.

The fact remained that Lina had no inevitable and legitimate employment. As they lived in lodgings, she had not even the small domestic affairs of a first establishment to look after. Employment, grave or gay, is a necessity to the human subject, so Lina had to manufacture her own.   Through her staunch friend, Leila's, good offices, she had regained a sufficient circle of acquaintances, and these stood her in great stead.   It is extraordinary what will serve for a morning's employment to young women of this particular kind.   Still, upon such profound resources Lina and her allies joyfully drew, and physically flourished.

For a week or two after that memorable expedition Lina saw nothing of Mr. Charles Robson, and the fact began to weigh upon her.   An inquiry, however, relieved her, by apprising her of the fact that he had gone to Paris.   She thought he *might* have confided to her his intention ; but in due course he re-appeared one morning in Grainger Street as fascinating as ever. But he was in a hurry, and flitted like a sunbeam, to leave her again very much in the shadow. For the rest of that day, Lina was in a most irritable condition. She thought that even a hurry might have been put aside for her after a fortnight's absence, and she determined to show him so on the next occasion of their meeting. She had a quarrel with her husband that night.

The next day chanced to be a wet one, and Lina did not go out. As she lay on the sofa in the afternoon, reading the literature of her own selection, she was vaguely aware of wheels having stopped suddenly outside, but to such an ordinary occurrence she naturally paid no attention. Footsteps up to her own door, however, followed, and for no definite reason a thrill of excitement passed through her as she laid down her book.

"Mr. Robson, m'm," she heard uttered in the

familiar voice of the servant, and before she could leap from her place, Mr. Robson himself was before her.

" Pray don't move. Isn't your husband at home ? Oh, I'm so sorry."

Having heard these words, the servant closed the door behind her. Lina got up in confusion, conscious of her red-hot blushes, and ignorant of their cause.

" I should have told you yesterday, if you hadn't been in *such* a hurry, that he is now engaged in a bank."

" Really ! . . . I was awfully sorry yesterday. In fact, I half came to-day to apologise."

" I don't think I shall forgive you."

" Oh, please ! "

" Well, will you come in to-morrow evening ? "

" Really couldn't, unless Mr. Crozier—I positively must meet him, you know. You know what a place this is."

" Oh, I mean to meet my husband, of course. He really shall be here this time."

" I shall be delighted. About six ? . . . A little

later, very good." And in a few minutes Lina was listening to the wheels departing.

She lay down to her book again, but it was a long time before she could attend to her reading.

Sibbald always came in fatigued or disgusted from his mechanical labours, and consequently not in the best of tempers. However, when he appeared to-night, he found Lina in such a sprightly, propitiating humour that he almost at once relaxed.

"It must be horrid at first; but you'll get used to it. After your life on the hills it must seem very, very horrid."

"But it's absurd, ridiculous, insane," exploded Crozier, more vehemently than he had allowed himself of late. "Do you call this a human existence when there's the bent and heather to live upon? You might as well go and live in a coal mine."

"But, dearie, others think of those dreadfully lonely hills just like you think of the town," pleaded Lina, with exceptional logic.

" I suppose they do," laughed Sibbald. " You did, anyway. But I am jolly certain I shall soon die here."

"Oh, Sib ! . . . Don't be angry ; but if you would only enjoy yourself like others do, you would find it all so different."

" But what if it's no enjoyment to you ? "

" It might be in time. If you would make friends like other young men—"

" Mr. Charles Robson, I suppose, for instance."

" Why not Mr. Charles Robson ? " retorted Adelina, resenting the tone he used. " He is a thorough gentleman, and I'm sure he would put you into good spirits if you have any good spirits left in you. And he reads, too. He is studying for the bar."

This served Lina more than she could have suspected, for to Sibbald's elementary notions it was also impressive.

" Is he ? Why, he must be quite a learned fellow," said he reflectively.

" He is a learned fellow ; but he doesn't let his

learning crush all the fun out of his life. Let me ask him here to-morrow night, and you can judge for yourself. He was so disappointed last time that he couldn't see you."

"Certainly ask him here."

"You will really see him?"

"Why shouldn't I see him?"

This was by no means the artful victory that Adelina thought it. For a day or two Sibbald had been revolving this very subject of making some friends for himself, in view of the unsatisfactory re-sult of his advances to Daniel Curle. It was difficult for Crozier to persuade himself that his instinctive dislike and distrust of his wife's social atmosphere could be all fallacious; but his late victory over himself in several particulars had succeeded in modifying his attitude in others. He was, therefore, fully prepared to submit to an interview with this parti-cular favourite, Mr. Robson, in order to judge more closely for himself, and, if at all possible, to advance to still further self-conquests in his company.

Adelina's excitement knew no bounds, for she considered that if this new connection were effected, her own intercourse with Mr. Robson would be so greatly simplified and, at the same time, extended. He would often come to the house. Almost weekly excursions could be planned into the country, and in the woods with Charlie Robson had proved itself to be one of the most ecstatic pleasures which social life could give to Lina.

The following evening, therefore, was no ordinary one either for Lina or her husband. The latter managed to get home in good time, and before the visitor had appeared. For this the wife was befittingly grateful, and she fluttered about him in a manner not usual of late days. At about a quarter to seven Mr. Robson arrived.

He greeted Sibbald with profuse cordiality, putting on that frank familiarity common between young men of an age, if also just a spice of superiority. Crozier smelt scent, and saw little but tie and waistcoat. Charlie was strong in ties and waistcoats, varying the hue of both more than once a day.

" I'm glad to see you—at last," was all Sibbald could say with a smile, and that with difficulty.

It was a fine sunny evening, so at the visitor's suggestion the three of them went off to the Park. Robson sniffed what he had expected, in his own facetious words, " a superior young man." It wasn't a young man he affected, so he felt that open air was preferable. This suited Sibbald also, and they went off in good spirits.

By way of commencement, Robson launched upon a full and entertaining account of a day trip to Holy Island, which he had taken at Easter, and which had no particular relevance to their present meeting, but which afforded him unlimited running material for talk. In that it relieved him of all responsibility Sibbald was quite content, and though he couldn't share the mirth which Charlie's sparkling humour kept alive in Adelina, he sustained himself creditably. Still, it required but a very short time to convince him that if Mr. Charles Robson was to be the only present aid to the self-conquest he contemplated, the said self-conquest was doomed not to be.

Within the enclosure Robson paused a moment to offer his cigar-case to his companion. The latter did not smoke, so declined.

" But you will, Mr. Robson," interposed Lina. "Oh, please do."

" You really don't object ? "

" Why, you know I like it."

On coming to a vacant seat, they sat down, and still Mr. Robson's voice and Lina's giggle continued very much in the ascendant. Sibbald put in a commonplace word or two now and then, and the speaker from time to time addressed his words directly to Lina, but it was not difficult to see that Crozier was practically not of the party. Up above the town here, with a north-west wind, the evening was lovely, and, in accordance with a life-long habit, the Scholar's eyes and mind were turned to the merely natural conditions. The echoing cuckoo and the little chiff-chaff in the bushes near at hand, were the voices that mainly engaged him : the yellowing sky and the tinted clouds amidst it, what he mainly saw. Thus left to his own reflections, a melancholy gradually crept over him, an intolerable suggestion of other scenes. He saw that brilliant light being lifted up the hill-sides by the shadows which were settling on the valleys, and heard the moorland sounds re-echoing in that awful stillness. Nay, perhaps he saw also a radiant image illumined by that golden light on a threshold facing west ; but if so, his gaze was quickly averted. That, at least, was no longer a sight for him, even in remote imagination.

" Don't you think so, Crozier ? "

Perhaps it was jocosely done ; at any rate, Robson

and Adelina laughed at the glance he turned to them, and Sibbald himself thawed into a smile.

"I was in the hills," said he frankly. "It will be glorious there to-night. But what were you asking?"

As Crozier listened to the repetition of Robson's remark, he looked about him consciously. Many other figures were moving to and fro, and he cast his eyes carelessly over them. Two men at a little distance excited his instant attention, he hardly knew why. One was smoking a pipe, and the other had at that instant turned his back towards them. The smoker said something to his companion, and then moved away, when Sibbald at once saw that it was Daniel Curle. Crozier was aware that the latter had seen and recognised him, and as there was an uncertainty in his movements, he did not remove his eyes. A minute or two was enough to convince Sibbald that the man meditated speaking to him, and himself, only too glad of an opportunity of escape even for a moment, took the initiative.

" Excuse me, will you ? " said he, rising. " There's a man I want to see." And Sibbald walked directly across to Daniel, to the supreme astonishment of his two companions.

"Going to bolt again," muttered Mr. Robson humorously, ostensibly to himself, but loud enough for Adelina.

There was a singular display of diffidence in Curle's reception of his friend. He admitted that he had thought of approaching Crozier, but didn't like to interrupt him. However, if he was at liberty, would he take a little walk with him ? There was a subject to which he should like to direct his attention.

Altogether Daniel's behaviour surprised Sibbald. The overbearing assurance which had always characterised him was entirely absent, and a very unnatural hesitation had taken its place.

" Have you seen your father lately ? " he asked, to which he got the bluntest negative.

"No, no, of course not," Daniel pursued. "I happen often to have seen him lately at the Tynedale Club, and do you know I'm afraid he's going wrong; he's getting quite reckless, and will break up his constitution, for he's not a young man."

"And why should you tell me this now?" demanded the other, bursting into a passion. "I suppose you have known it ever since he came into the town, as I have done. What's your object in telling me when you know I am powerless? What have you to gain?"

This was just the attitude to rectify any uncertainty in Daniel, and his tone became firmer.

"It is scarcely likely that I have anything to gain beyond the satisfaction of having tried to help you."

"How? How? Tell me something definite, practical, and don't infuriate me with words."

"I think I can do that if you will only have a little patience."

"Then stay for me a moment."

It was a heaven-sent opportunity.

Sibbald strode back to the seat where he had left his two companions. As he approached, their laughter came to him and pierced him like steel. In any case he felt he could not again have joined them, so remote had that vision of the hills hurled him from them.

"I am sorry that again I shall have to leave you," said he quickly as he extended his hand to Robson. "I have to go down into the town. You will kindly see my wife home. . . . My father's affairs," he added, looking into Adelina's astonished face, and with a curt good-bye he was again on his way to Daniel.

"Didn't I say so?" chuckled Mr. Robson. . . . "But shall we walk a little? You'll find it chilly."

And they took the opposite way.

CHAPTER II.

UNDERCURRENTS.

"WAS that Felton with you just now?" asked Sibbald, as he and Curle walked onwards at a brisk pace. The speaker's eyes were fixed upon the ground, so he did not see how the question affected his companion.

"Yes, it was," replied Daniel after just the fraction of a pause. "And it is in connection with him that I want to speak to you."

"How has he got out of my father's clutches?"

"I help him to escape occasionally for fresh air. . . . Now, look here, Crozier, I want to be frank with you," continued Curle, assuming more of his old manner. "I have got the notion that only by removing Felton can we assist your father. So long as he has that man constantly under his nose he is kept in this preposterous condition. I only want your consent to it, and I can help him to escape altogether. The man is willing now to go abroad, and with the help of a friend I can enable him to do so. What do you say?"

Sibbald was silent for an instant. He felt an irresistible conviction that his companion was dissembling with him, yet he knew not why he should.

"Send him away by all means."

. "So I thought would be your decision," Curle went on, gathering confidence. "Well now, my idea is this. This man once away, you and I will have to act jointly. Suppose we appoint next Tuesday for a commencement. There is a boat goes to Copenhagen that day, and I can get Felton quietly on board. They would never think of hunting in that direction, you see. I will also make sure that your father is detained at the club until eight o'clock, when I will come up home with him, and—and will you be hanging about to meet us as we go in ? "

" I fail to see what good I shall be. He refuses intercourse with me."

" He has done, it is true ; but I will do my utmost to prepare him. If he refuses to ask you in that night, well, we shall have made the attempt. I, in any case, shall go in with him, so that he won't make the discovery of Felton's escape alone. That would be impossible. We might have a tragedy. Action after that must depend upon circumstances. I could see you again, and we could consult."

Sibbald could not for the life of him see any drift to the argument, but he attributed it to his own con-fusion, for he knew that he was all but distracted. At anyrate it would be doing *something* in the matter, so he gave a general assent.

" The great object is to keep the coast clear for Felton's escape, and that, of course, must depend largely upon me. If I should find it absolutely necessary to change the day I will let you know, but I do not anticipate this. If you hear nothing from me do not fail to be up there at eight o'clock. If we can possibly work it we ought to get the old man out of the town. That is the end I work for, but the means are not altogether so clear. Here he will go direct to perdition."

" He wishes to," assented Crozier vehemently.

" Ay, ay, but we'll see about it. If he's worked the right way something may yet be done. Tuesday night at eight, then ? "

" But you are not going ? " said Crozier in surprise. " I will walk down with you—"

"There is nothing I should like better than a long talk, but now it is impossible. Felton is waiting for me, and any accident now will upset all. If I had not so fortunately seen you I meant to call. This is better. Good-night."

Curle forthwith darted off in a most erratic manner, and left Sibbald to wonder whether the world was stable about him. Acting upon his former preoccupation, the man seemed to have burst unintelligibly upon him, and beyond eight o'clock on Tuesday night he could have given no coherent account of the proposition intended to have been made to him. That impression of Curle's duplicity, too, intensified the haze in which everything was enfolded, so that he strode forward in a state of unusual bewilderment, and quite regardless of his steps.

Daniel soon recovered his companion Felton, and seemed to show high displeasure.

" You'll wreck it all," he vociferated, " and—and I'll give you up if you do. You ken what's in store for you, my man—"

"Has he undertaken to do it?" asked Felton calmly.

" He has promised to meet him at his door," replied Daniel, fixing his teeth. "And he is favourable to your escape."

" Very good. Do you think I'll have his very life on my soul ? "

" Well, come along.   Can't you see the time ? "

By a hurried cross route, with scarce a word on the journey, they came to the house which old Crozier occupied, and Felton was let in.   Then Curle went on into the town with a fixed expression of anger on his features.

What he considered his confederate's sentimental requirements enraged Daniel, and in these days he was excessively irritable.   He went directly to the Tynedale Club, and there he found old Crozier. The latter hailed him immediately, and they went into a private corner together.

" Hae ye the cash, man ? " said the elder with some urgency.

" Cash ?   No, it is to be completed on Tuesday. I have got them definitely to fix the day.   But they want you to be present."

" Eh, what !   The thieves !   Did aa'd Elliott say sae ? "

" He did."

" Then ye may tell him frae me that I'll see him and his three thousand damned fawst."

" He says you ought to have employed a lawyer." There was almost a twinkle in Curle's eyes as he awaited the result of this politic stroke of his.

" And did you no tell him that I'd rather gan into the Tyne with a brick to my thrapple, than ever deal wi' the like o' yon again?" he demanded, almost choking with passion. "Arena the writings in order? Have ye no done it for 'em as good as any thief on Tyneside could hae done it? But I ken him—I ken him nicely. He wants to insult me; he wants—"

His voice was getting too high, so Curle put his hand on his arm.

" No, no; they have to look after themselves, that's all. If you object to see him. . . . Ssh! . . . He'll pay it over to me if you write and sign an authority for him to do so."

" Why couldna you tell me that at fawst? . . .

Come away, and I'll write it the noo. . . . What'll I put, man ? "

They went to a table forthwith, and procuring stationery, the old man wrote what Daniel dictated. When it was done, Mr. Crozier's temper subsided, and they talked in a calmer vein. But Curle did not stay long. His restlessness improvised another engagement. After he had left Crozier he returned to him again.

" I forgot to say that I shall be out of town for a day or two," he said to him. " If I don't see you again before Tuesday, I'll call here for you at seven-thirty p.m. that day. We shall just be up to give the poor devil his feed by eight."

Crozier laughed, and dismissed him. The feed referred to a humorous suggestion of Daniel's which had tickled the old man extremely. It was to celebrate the sale of Bygate by a champagne supper to Felton (to be prepared by himself) on the day the cash was received. This had previously been fixed for eight o'clock. So Daniel went.

But, to his amazement, in the street outside he met Sibbald, who was making for the club doorway.

" Is my father there ? "

" My dear fellow—"

" Is he there, I say ? "

" He is ; but if you disturb him now you'll put an end to all our plans."

Crozier's excitement was obvious, and this seemed to check him.

" Why, is he drunk ? "

" Not exactly ; but he is in a furious temper. . . . But go and see." And Curle hurried away.

Needless to say that Sibbald did not go and see. He had only come here on impulse, worked up by his reflections since leaving the Park, and this check came in time to show him the absurdity of what he was about. He had resolved upon an instant inter-view with his father for one supreme effort to get

him to leave the town at once. After the incidents
of that evening, the youth was overwhelmed by the
conviction that for himself, no less than for his
father, refuge alone lay in departure from the town.
It seemed to him in that mood that even for the
prosecution of his own designs this was the inevitable
course, for although thousands of pounds were undoubtedly made in the town more speedily than
elsewhere, how was *he* to set to work to make them?
At present he was in receipt of something over fifty
pounds a year, and he had already obtained his
fellow juniors' ideas upon the subject of promotion.
He could sooner gather three thousand pounds by
herding sheep than by his savings in this new
calling.

But this practical calculation had only come as an
after thought. It was the spiritual requirements
which mainly actuated him. The impression of Mr.
Charles Robson oppressed him like a nightmare, for
with characteristic absurdity he considered *him* to

typify the prospects of urban civilisation. Not only
had he found that vaunted friend to be exactly what
he had expected, but he could not fail to perceive
how his own wife shone by the side of him, as
though catching a tinsel brilliance from the kindred
quality of polish. This re-awakened the very depths
of Sibbald's savage discontent.

After seeing Daniel, he resolved to delay his action
until he was in a calmer frame of mind. But he
could not at once go home, from the fear that
Robson would not yet have left. So he roamed
about, endeavouring to reduce his disordered energies
to some clear and possible method.

" Here you are ! " exclaimed Lina with a yawn
when he came in and found her on the sofa. " I
thought perhaps you were going to be away for the
night again."

" A pity I didn't think of it before," replied he, for
he was irritated beyond endurance by that unfortunate yawn. " Has Mr. Robson gone?"

There was no response, and he proceeded to take off his boots. Then he called for some supper, and he ate voraciously in silence.

When he rose from the table his nerves were calmer, but his resolution remained unchanged.

"I didn't much care for your friend, Lina," he said, handling something on the mantelpiece. "So I might as well tell you the truth. I shouldn't like you to see him very often."

This came like a pistol shot to Adelina, and however drowsy before, she was instantly alert enough. She simply opened her eyes widely and stared at him. She could not find a single word to utter. The tone equally with the matter amazed her.

"That isn't the kind of life I wish you to get into."

"All right, all right. I don't want a sermon. You can choose your own friends, and I'll choose mine."

Lina was sorry for the hasty words when they were uttered, but she wouldn't recall them, and she was really very angry. For a farmer indeed—a man who had passed all his life with books and sheep on the side of a desolate mountain—to talk thus of Mr. Charles Robson of Newcastle, Paris and elsewhere! That closed the conversation ; neither of them spoke another word that night.

The incident was useful to Sibbald, for it served to concentrate his emotions upon his own domestic situation. The shock, moreover, put an edge to his resolution, and he acted with a promptitude characteristic of former rather than late days. He had fully intended to discuss amicably with his wife this thought of returning to the country, but he intended it no more. When his arrangements were completed he should announce to her the result. He considered that he had unsuccessfully tried one method ; he would now try another.

The very next day he set about an inquiry for obtainable hill farms. The time of year was not favourable, but some casualty might possibly aid him. So indeed he found ; for the names of two were given him, one relinquished through bankruptcy, the other through death. The former was situated on the north Tyne; the latter in Rede water. It was to this latter that Sibbald inclined, for the actual place was known to him, and slightly the deceased farmer.

On the Saturday following Crozier obtained leave of absence, and went away to inspect the place. He still did not confide his purpose to Adelina, simply remarking in the morning that he should be absent all day. When he returned at night he was the accepted tenant of Whaupriggs.

The expedition convinced him that he was on the right track. In such marked contrast to his futile attempts at finding employment in the town, as he inspected the farm he found his mind fall into the congenial groove immediately, and all the technical possibilities rise up before him in instinctive association with the ground. So much hay to that lower field; so much turnips and oats to this. So many score sheep over that headland, and so many more over the other. His calculations were made in a moment, and the place known to be within the capabilities of his purse and judgment. Out there, too, his vision became clearer in several general respects. Calmly but firmly should he deal with Adelina. She should by no means be a servant to him, but in sufficient pleasant employment she should certainly be engaged. He could see all the injury to her character from the unemployed days. Though undoubtedly it would be a blow to her at first, the radical alteration in her existence would ultimately develop what was best. As he looked over the sunlit lea he could admit no shadow of a doubt of it. His father did not offer quite so clear a solution, but—this one last effort should be made with him, and then the fates must direct. With something almost approaching his old buoyancy, therefore, he set foot again in the town, at least in the station, for as he came amidst the throng of passengers from his own train on to the main platform, something again occurred to assail his new-born spirits.

A similar throng was also coming from a train on the other side of the station, and amongst the foremost of them to meet his eyes who should appear but his wife, Adelina, and Mr. Charles Robson, advancing in company. The sight this time threw him into a tremulous agitation; not of anger, but of a sickening inarticulate dread. It was as though something had fallen from his eyes, and he had beheld a horrible apparition. He shrank back, hiding himself behind his neighbours, to watch them pass beneath the block; the sound of his wife's laughter, and, he thought, the fumes of Robson's cigar, reaching him as they went. He had one more glimpse of them driving away in a cab, and then he was in the street alone.

Not as a woman, but as a ghostly spectre rather, had Adelina appeared to him. The halo of his own ideal womanhood had never hitherto fully left her, even through their troubled days, but now she was a skeleton. Shameless impudence gleamed out of her hollow eye-sockets, and abandoned glee rattled from her throat. He tried to shut his eyes to the spectacle, but it was upon his brain and heart that it was imprinted.

It was almost an hour before he reached his lodgings. When at length he entered he found Lina standing by the chimney-piece, and she turned towards him with her lips apart for some vivacious sally, but the words did not come. He gave one look into her face, ghastly pale as he noticed, and then he lowered his eyes.

" Sib ! "

But she stopped on seeing there were tears in his eyes, and that he was struggling ineffectually to speak. He also raised a hand to warn her back. Then the blood rushed to her face, and hiding it in her hands, she fell upon the sofa sobbing.

" I—I w-won't see him again ! . . . I won't see

him again ! " she twice exclaimed in broken accents, and she could speak no more.

Some time later Lina, with swollen eyes and dis-figured features, lay upon the sofa, nibbling the fringe of her fancy apron, and listening to her husband's cold enunciation of his plans. He revealed the ob-ject of his journey that day, and of the result of it. So soon as he could get the necessary preparations completed, they would move to this farm that he had taken and—and try to begin afresh. It was a plain, matter-of-fact statement. No fervent depicting of an ideal life under these new circumstances. It was uttered rather in the tone of one who has begun to suspect that the key of existence lies in passive en-durance rather than in active buoyant hope, that to him that expecteth nothing, cometh no disappoint-ment. Upon his hearer, too, the effect seemed to be similarly spiritless. There was no spark of resistance to be traced in her, scarcely of comprehension.

" When shall we go ? " she asked listlessly, after

Sibbald had been explaining what preparations he had to make.

"As soon as I can do all this," repeated he, glancing at her. "In not more than three weeks I hope."

"Yes."

It was only in the course of the next day or two that Lina awoke to the fact of all it signified to her. Throughout the Sunday she was noticeably dejected, and did not leave the house. Sibbald, on the other hand, found it impossible to remain within doors. It required nothing less than the bosom of the natural world to sustain the ills which were now befalling him. Even the condition of his father sank into insignificance before this hideous peril surrounding Adelina, and which had been so suddenly revealed to his unsuspecting eyes. He found some small consolation in the fact that even she was now evidently aware of her danger, and in her emphatic resolution to shun it entirely for the future. But that it could ever assail her! That was enough to poison the very springs of spiritual life for him.

Lina's Sabbath reflection did not all result from the burden of her frivolous behaviour. It chanced that she had parted from Mr. Robson with a definite engagement for this coming week, and, in spite of her vehement declaration, now in the light of another day, it was not so easily decided whether, at least, she ought not to see him just to say that she could not come. Over this, when alone, she shed many bitter tears, and still remained in an agony of indecision. The next day, however, decided it for her.

In the afternoon she went out, and at the first street corner met Mr. Robson in person. Raising his hat, he simply walked on beside her.

"I—I really can't come," she stammered.

"No, I know," he replied in his airiest manner. "I saw Mr. Crozier this morning."

She turned a look of terror upon him, and he chuckled.

" Don't be alarmed. You see he didn't shoot me. He is really a remarkable fellow, and has an astounding selection of language."

"You didn't quarrel with him? It's cruel—"

" No, no; he only quarrelled with me. I never quarrel on principle; least of all with a man who has a sweetly pretty wife that he uses abominably. . . . But really I shall have to look in the dictionary for some of the words he applied to me."

" Just like him!" cried Adelina hotly. "And— and he's taken another farm!"

The outer corners of Mr. Robson's eyelids were naturally a little depressed, and when he wanted to assume a peculiarly arch expression he had the power of lowering them a little further. So he did now.

" But surely you're not troubled about that. Dairy and poultry in the wilderness! what can possibly be more delightful? No disturbance to one's reflection. Upon my word I'd a good mind to follow suit, but—I can't get a pretty wife to come and help me."

"Don't be, silly!" said Lina, with some severity, but aware of a gratifying increase of strength under his banter. "But I really sha'n't come on Wednesday."

"No, no, of course not,—far better not." She looked at him with a puzzled expression.

"Now, which do you mean? I believe you don't want me." Charlie shrugged his shoulders.

"Do nothing rashly," said he sententiously. "I just met you here to tell you of the meeting this morning, and that he's forbidden me the door. So Q. T., you understand?"

"But do you think I ought to come?"

"Follow your own judgment. *We* shall go anyway. Ta-ta!"

She couldn't detain him, so she took an abrupt turning and came to the Park. There she spent all the afternoon in wild, irreconcilable thought.

Reflection or cogitation were words inapplicable to Adelina, for the states they signify were not possible to her. She couldn't think in any strict sense of the term. She was simply swayed this way and that by variable, irresponsible impulses. So it was now. She had some conception of what the world calls right and wrong, and, on the whole, she would have preferred to keep to the right had conflicting fancies permitted her to take that course. However, she found herself possessed of the notion that in a solitary farm-house like Bygate she should die, and it seemed to her that her life was of such superlative value that *that* conclusion was really not to be thought of. " Oh, how can I possibly go out there again ? . . . And with him ? " This was the constant burden of her thoughts, to which she was ever returning. . . . And what if she didn't go out there with him ? But that corollary would have been logical, therefore one at which Lina was by no means likely to arrive. As a matter of fact, she did not arrive at it. She simply sated her fancy with the intolerable first propositions. Therefore, after some hours wandering, she reached home in a state of rebellious irresolution. Rebellious, however, it undoubtedly was, and so showed that one step had been taken. The passionate remorse of Saturday night had been routed by wholly antagonistic forces, making remorse weaker and less likely in future, and its enemy stronger and very much more likely.

Sibbald did not mention to her his meeting with Robson, and that again embittered her, for it was a clear proof to her of the continuance of that old-standing duplicity. If he did not trust her, how could she him? Adelina's ethics did not permit of any loftier, more independent line of argument than this. Indeed, she noted altogether a very distinct change in his attitude. He could not even pretend to act that tenderness upon which he had relied formerly. That ghastly vision at the station had effectually killed that. The sacrilege *now* would have been to bestow even the semblance of what was due only to his ideal upon one who had displayed herself so alien from that sacred trust. Simply a tragical determination marked his behaviour, and he spoke of everything purely from a matter-of-fact standpoint.

The next day passed, and although Lina went out with the definite intention of again invoking the serious counsel of Mr. Robson, she had been unable to meet him. The approach of Wednesday put her into a high commotion, for every moment it became more clear that the decision must come unreservedly from herself. In all Lina's actions she preferred to have some direct influence from without upon which she could feel to be leaning. Just at this perhaps most critical moment of her existence it was to be denied her.

Sibbald was out that evening (it was Tuesday), and in her agonies of attempted self-reliance Lina snatched at this fact as a guiding string in the chaos. Even still he went off enjoying himself, whilst he not only left her at home to mope, but he took low and violent measures to deprive her of the few only pleasures that her life otherwise had. Was it right? Was it possible that she could exist like that? Men did what they liked, but if a woman did, they could not find names bad enough for her in the dictionary. It wasn't fair. What one might do, the other might—or at anyrate would. This once more at least she would go, if only to assert her independence. If that dear foolish Charlie *should* " carry on " as he did last Saturday,— well, she would have to be cross with him, and per- haps refuse ever to go again.

Her husband's appearance fully confirmed her resolve. He came in at about nine o'clock, and had more pointedly than ever left all his mirth behind him.

" I think I shall be able to get off earlier than I thought—perhaps next week."

She found it difficult to be civil, and there was

more than her usual indifference in the assent she gave. Silence again fell. Lina pretended to be reading.

"Did you know that your father had gone abroad?"

" Has he gone?   I heard that he thought of going."

Even some amount of interest was excited in her by this remark.

" He has gone, but I don't know where to." Sibbald marvelled at the " I heard," so carelessly uttered, but at once recognised it as merely further evidence of the width of their estranged life.   In all probability, he thought, she knew far more about many things than he did.   So he was again silent.

In a minute or two he got up and walked restlessly about the room.   The trouble on his features now irritated Lina, as she furtively glanced at him, rather than excited sympathy or regret.   Yes, his all—all the responsibility !   Had he been open with her,— been different in so many ways—none of this would ever have happened.

" Look here, Lina," exclaimed Crozier abruptly

from one end of the table, "you don't care a pin for these new plans I am making. You don't take a scrap of interest in my life. You haven't even asked to go and see this place that is to be our new home. If you don't want to see it, if you don't want to go, you might at least make some little pretence that you do. We shall have to live our life I suppose, now we have undertaken it. Will you come with me to Redesdale to-morrow?"

Lina was stricken dumb by the amazing suggestion, and simply stared at her book.

"You can at least tell me what you would like to do with the rooms. I can't spend much on furniture, but what I can spend might as well be spent in what you like as in what you won't like."

"B-but I can't possibly go to-morrow," faltered she.

"Oh, all right. Perhaps you will tell me when you can."

Lina didn't answer, and so the subject was abandoned for the night.

CHAPTER III.

"Give me the gold, good John o' Scales,
And thine for aye my land shall be."

THAT was Tuesday night, and, in accordance with his promise to Daniel, Sibbald had been near the door of his father's house before eight o'clock. It happened that he had met Curle casually that morning, and had confided to him his tenancy of the farm.

"Excellent!" cried Daniel, although in a great hurry. "Just the thing! we'll get him there. Patience, patience, and we'll do it. To-night at eight."

Curle's action upon Crozier varied. That morning it proved to be the provocative, so Sibbald acquiesced in the hurry, and passed on.

As Daniel went down the street after this, a curious nervous smile played about his features. His appointment for completing the Bygate transaction was for twelve o'clock at Mr. Elliott's office, and the intervening hours were spent by Curle not in any other business but in flitting about the Quayside and its neighbourhood, with a black bag, making inquiries at this and that shipping office. He seemed absorbed in business. Talked of this and that commercial transaction with acquaintances he met. When his watch showed a quarter to twelve, he went and took a ticket for the Copenhagen boat, then went up to Lord Braiddale's agent.

With him he was engaged but a few minutes, handing over the deed of conveyance, duly executed by Maxwell Crozier, together with the other deeds and documents relating to the Bygate property. The purchase money he counted, in large notes, transferred them to his bag in exchange for the written authority from the old man, and an additional receipt

signed by himself, which Mr. Elliott demanded.
This way of doing important business through under-
lings was not to his taste.   Therewith he bade Mr.
Curle good-day.

Daniel's watch showed six minutes past twelve ;
the Edinburgh train departed at 12.15.   Ample
time, for the station was close at hand, and he went
at once towards it.   In the covered archway, as he
entered, he met Felton.

"Booked ? " said Daniel.   "Go and get in, but
stand in the doorway."

Felton obediently passed through to the north
express, which was waiting, whilst his companion
went farther down the platform.

The few remaining minutes fled, and as the
ominous banging of the doors began, a passenger
stood on the step of a first-class compartment in
visible agitation.

" Take your seat, please, sir," said a porter hurrying
by.

" One minute, there's a—"

" Can't wait, sir."

But as Felton was thrust in, another gentleman
with a black bag darted from the railings, and was
on his heels. The door closed, and the train
started.

" Then he must miss it," muttered Felton between
his teeth, as he drew in his head from a last survey of
the platform.

" What are you growling at ? " came in response
from an inner corner in a voice which the other
seemed to recognise.

" Heavens alive ! " And, distraught as he was,
Felton burst into a prolonged peal of laughter.

Daniel's disguise was evidently consummate, for
Felton was under the impression that it was a
stranger who had got into his carriage. He stared
and stared again at the trim, close-cut brown beard ;
held out his fingers to examine it ; laughed and
laughed again.

"All right, that'll do," said Curle impatiently.
" You left all square ? "

" I shall look to you, Daniel—"

The other interrupted him by handing across the
Copenhagen ticket. Felton looked inquiringly at
him, for he had not been entrusted with any of his
confederate's arrangements. What Daniel had told
him to do he had done. He now raised his eyebrows.

" But this is from here. Does the boat go on to
Leith ? " Curle scarcely disguised his impatient
contempt.

" That's where we're gone to anyway . . . with
that, and possibly Antwerp or Amsterdam, the scent
is broken. I've been parading the quay all the
morning. I don't think there's any clue with the
station. I didn't see anybody about. I saw the
old man this morning. He's right till night. By then
we shall be—"

At Morpeth they procured papers, and hardly
exchanged a word for the rest of their journey.

The evening of that day was unsettled, showers having begun late in the afternoon. Sibbald found himself in but indifferent mood for the errand he was on, as he walked to and fro in the main thoroughfare, upon which his father's street abutted. He saw the great rolling clouds scudding over to the sea, and instinctively traced them to the lonely heights in the west from which they had travelled. When a gust of wind came, almost taking his hat away with it, his eyes lit up as he heard it wuthering down the Foulburn Knowe. But despite such meditations he kept an eager look-out along the pavement by which the pair must come. He could not but give a thought sometimes to Curle, and the object he must have in view. His satisfaction with him had not increased, and he had found it utterly impossible to believe that pure sympathy actuated this latest suggestion. But Sibbald had some confidence in his own powers of observation, and, his suspicions once aroused, he considered it would require an exceptional amount of ingenuity in Curle to impose upon him to any serious extent. It was clear enough that his father, just now, lent himself only too completely to imposition of various sorts, so that it was just possible that his own outside glance might enable him to detect and frustrate Daniel's intention.

Sped apparently by a scud of wind and rain, at length his father hove in sight, but, to Sibbald's surprise, he was alone. His step was in great contrast to the dignified pace assumed when his son had last seen him. Now the old man's eyes were fixed upon the pavement, and although dressed as carefully as ever, he wore nothing to protect him from the beating rain. He suggested at that moment the old shepherd stalking over the hills, rather than the character he had lately been assuming. Sibbald regulated his own pace so as to intercept his father at the corner. As he confronted him the old man looked up.

" Dan—" But as if collecting his senses, he stopped

and required some seconds to recognise his adver-sary.

"It's no you, but Daniel Curle I want; hae you seen him?"

"I saw him this morning, and he told me to meet him with you here at eight o'clock."

"Here? . . . He told me the club," muttered the elder, looking away; but then suddenly altering his manner, he exclaimed, "Well, come away, man; ye were a Crozier yae day if ye arena the noo. Come away ben, and ye'll hae a drappit wi' us the night, onyway. It's no just an ordinar' occasion, ye ken; Daniel 'ull be here, belive, I'se warr'nd. Come away, come away!"

In supreme astonishment, Sibbald followed him to the door in silence, and they went in. Just shaking himself like a dog and throwing down his hat, the old man went into the room at the back.

"Ay, ay, that'll dea. . . . Come in here, man!" he called to Sibbald, who had lingered in the passage.

As he entered, the youth saw the table spread in a comparatively elaborate manner with excess of glass, silver, and cutlery. On the old side-board, so familiar to him in other quarters, stood a whole regiment of champagne, as well as of bottles of spirits. It was evident that some high feast was in contemplation, and he doubted not at the expense of the patrimonial acres. Leaving him there to examine it all at leisure, the former went to the head of the kitchen steps and shouted for Felton. Sibbald did not catch the reply; in fact, the lifeless silence of the house had oppressed the young man from the moment of entering. There was the sound of footsteps descending to the lower regions, but still no ensuing conversation was audible, and Sibbald did not suppose his father was a man to converse in whispers. He himself thought of "Copenhagen," and prepared himself for the altered attitude. The steps re-ascended, but passed his door, and went on to the general staircase. Breathless, Sibbald listened to the old man going silently from room to room upstairs, the sounds his feet made, and the opening of doors, re-echoing through the house. But there were no voices. After exploring every corner of the house, the steps came down again.

The alteration in his father was not exactly what Sibbald had expected. He re-entered, not the blind, infuriate farmer breathing out vengeance against all mankind, but the cold, dignified, self-restrained old gentleman that the youth had encountered on a former occasion. Without speaking, he uncorked a bottle of champagne, poured out a glass for his visitor, and one for himself, the latter of which he drank at a draught, and filled the glass again. Then he took out his watch.

"What time do you make it by your watch?" he asked.

" A quarter past eight," said the other.

" Then I needn't keep you. We'll no have our celebration the night." Sibbald looked at him, but could not gain his eye.

" Now I am here, father, I might as well tell you that I am going back to the country. I have taken Whaupriggs, up the Rede water."

"That's no concern o' mine, sir. You're at liberty to take Whaupriggs, or any other riggs—and—and be damned to ye!"

" And if you'll come up any day,—perhaps for a Sunday, to look round—"

" Ay, ay, but it's no that likely," interposed the old man, exercising, as it seemed, some extraordinary power over himself, and signalling his visitor to the door.

" But if you—"

" I'll no come, I tell you. . . . Get out o' the hoose without another wawd."

For an hour there was no sound in the house, except the slow ticking of the old clock, and the measured pace of old Crozier walking from the room into the passage, from the passage into the room again. Daniel did not come.

The point had come at which the disappearance of Felton alone would have had but very little effect upon the man. So very many new distractions had risen up for him, that that old fixed idea of enjoying daily the humiliation of the man who had imposed upon him, and to whom he attributed all his disorders, had waned almost to extinction. The thought had once or twice of late occurred to him of dismissing the fellow, as a source of growing annoyance rather than of satisfaction, and it was by no means impossible that this night, which was to celebrate the downfall of .Bygate, should also have thrown Felton at large upon the world again. That such had been a vague intention was, in Maxwell Crozier's philosophy, however, by no means a mitigation of the blow of the discovery. It added to its force a thousand fold, under the circumstances of this evening. Had not the man triumphed once more over him ?

The subject, moreover, served but as a foil to a darker and deeper disorder behind. During that

hour of pacing to and fro, Crozier was vituperating
Felton, but also assuring himself, with characteristic
oaths, that Daniel's absence signified nothing at all.
Curle was a man of affairs; had constantly enraged
him beyond endurance by his unpunctuality and
disregard of appointments—but to-night! As the old
man had told his son, the occasion was no just
ordinar', and, with three thousand pounds in your
pocket, Daniel's customary haunts were not exactly
the places to be delayed in. At half-past nine the
front door was opened and shut, and Mr. Crozier was
in the street. He procured a cab, and drove first to
Daniel's lodgings. It chanced that the landlady herself came to the door, and she was frank. She admitted she didn't understand Mr. Curle. They had
always kept the best of terms, and yet, when he
wanted to leave, he couldn't speak out to her like a
man, and give her a reason. But will you just come
inside, sir? Old Crozier stepped inside, the perspiration dropping from his temples, and in the passage
,

under the lamp, the woman put a note into his hand, which she said had been delivered at two o'clock that day.

"Above all things, I do like to be straightforrard," she concluded, with some emphasis. "If he'd wanted to change, should I ha' grumbled? He's always paid punctual, and some gentlemen do like to change their lo-calities at times. But to go and pertend as he's left the town all of a hop like that—it's not reasonable. If he's not satisfied, let him 'a said so. . . ."

The perspiration poured from Mr. Crozier's eye-brows to his eyes, so that he had to clear his vision with his handkerchief to read the words.

"DEAR MRS. BLENKHORN,—I enclose postal order for twenty-five shillings, which I believe will square us up to next Saturday. I have also to tell you that I shall not want my rooms any longer, as most un-expectedly I have to leave the town this morning on important business, which may possibly lead to an appointment out of Newcastle altogether.—Yours truly, DANIEL CURLE."

"Did you want him very special, sir?" inquired the woman, as Crozier handed her the letter back without a word. "He did a lot of law business for folks. When my brother Wilkin died—"

"What's that to me, woman?" roared the old man, and swept out of the house immediately. He bade the cabman drive to the Tynedale Club.

Daniel had not been heard of there that night, since Mr. Crozier had been clamouring for him before. No inducement could detain the farmer there. He paid his cabman and walked up home.

He let himself into the dark house, and did not immediately strike a light. The ray from a lamppost outside penetrated the dark front room (corresponding to the old man's private parlour at Bygate), and had anybody been standing on the pavement to look, a grey-haired, motionless figure might have been discerned within it, the large black shadow of which was thrown over the old bureau by the wall. It is possible that if Sibbald had presented himself at this moment, a different reception might have awaited him. The farmer could no longer resist the appalling impression which was forced upon him, and he was smitten, stunned. For a long time he couldn't think coherently of anything about him—past, present, or to come. He felt detached, adrift on a chaotic world, utterly without sign or landmark. All the frenzied intentions which had actuated and restrained him hitherto, giving impulse and aim to his abandoned course, were extinguished, and he could not then have told you how he came to be there.

At length he sat in the armchair, with his eyes upon that gas-lamp outside, and he was still thus sitting when it was extinguished in the morning. But the daylight revived him a little, and he went out. He went to an hotel, and ordered breakfast,

and ate ravenously when it was before him.   He sat
there until ten o'clock.   As the clocks were striking,
he was once more in the street, presenting a singularly
altered aspect from the choleric old *gaillard* that had
left the Tynedale Club the previous night.   Not only
was his pace slow, but there was an uncertainty
about it, unknown after his most jovial sittings.   His
lips were tightly clenched, but nervously, and no
longer with that air of supreme defiance to all the
world, which had characterised him since he came to
the town.   He turned in at the office where Daniel
had been employed, and simply asked to see him.
One of the principals chanced to be in the clerk's
room, and he stated that Curle had left their employment on the Saturday previously at his own request.
He didn't know why, nor did he know where he had
gone.   The old man thanked him and went out.

" Then I'm dean," he muttered, as he left the building, and he again walked slowly up to his own house.

It was by no means old Crozier's instinctive im-

pulse to cry "Murder! Police!" He did not take
the smallest measures to trace the fugitive. The
humiliation was too great for that. As this day
wore on, it was this crushing, maddening humiliation
that formed the most articulate portion of his woe.
His arrogant pride was broken, shattered effectually.
There was not the smallest suspicion of rebound.
Some of this may possibly have arisen from a sense
of hopeless superiority in Curle. His former resentment of Felton's imposition upon him had been
instant and vehement ; but he had always despised
Felton. Towards Daniel Curle his attitude had been
one of childish subordination, almost abject recogni-
tion of what he considered to be superior parts, and
he was beaten. By mid-day, his principal terror was
that it might be found out, his only care to smother
it in the dark recesses of his own heart.

That it had been timed with the successful escape
of Felton could not appear a providential trick, for
confederacy did not for a moment suggest itself to

his mind.   If it had, it is just possible that the result might have been otherwise.

For the rest of that day, the old man did not go out.   On the following one he found a small measure of reaction, even a hint that Daniel *might* have been detained somewhere, and *might* communicate with him that day.   On the strength of that, he went down to the club again at lunch time ; but he found the atmosphere so stifling, and met with such a volley of raillery on his altered appearance, that he left before he had half finished.   He did not make the attempt again.   Crozier was quite aware of his change.   He knew that he ought to be breathing curses against the universe, meeting these plots against him with a double fist; but he also knew that he was physically incapable of it.   Any coherent thought was beyond him.   If he began to attempt to plan a course of action, the thread escaped him, and he got bewildered in the mazes of an unknown locality.   In a day or two, he began to roam about the house, muttering to himself, and peering into every corner as though in search of something. When he came to himself, he would stare strangely about him, ultimately having to look out of the window to gain the clue, and exclaim—

" But this is no Bygate, man. That's no Hawk-hope and Foulburn Knowe yonder—tarr'ble strange."

One morning he awoke in a clearer state, and leapt out of bed with vehement thoughts all distinct in his mind. Partially dressing himself, he went downstairs, talking loudly to himself as he descended.

" Ay, ay, it'll last a towmont onyway—rin it out, man, to the very hindmaist. My sartie, but I didna ken what to think on't. We'll dea the noo. One fifty, daur say, in the bank, and the Waggon Company will sell for five hundred or thereawa. We'll dea ; we'll dea."

He turned into his room with all the old vigour apparent in his step and features. Taking keys from his pocket he unlocked the bureau and pulled out some papers. When he had glanced at them, he threw them down and looked for more. He muttered impatiently, and pulled the things about in a reckless manner. At length he alighted on a long foolscap envelope, and took it up with satisfaction. On looking into it, however, he found it empty. His face coloured again deeply, and he dropped the paper.

Whilst he groped again tremulously amongst the papers he staggered and fell heavily to the floor.

CHAPTER IV.

CONFIDENCES.

SIBBALD gave himself up entirely to active preparation for flight. That refusal of Adelina to accompany him had stabbed him deeply, but had scarcely aroused any new emotion. He had gauged his life pretty accurately, and fully recognised that the aspirations of his own heart were dead, that the halo which was to him an essential attribute of married life no longer invested him. Daily facts must satisfy him henceforth.

So he went into Redesdale notwithstanding. After his former strong expression of opinion as to her associating with Robson, and his plain words to the man himself, Crozier was too proud to hint any inquiry as to Lina's engagement that day. She had several female acquaintances after her own kind, and it was no doubt to some of these that Sibbald in his mind allotted her on that occasion. He himself set off early, and simply announced that he should be back at night.

He had a busy day under exhilarating conditions. The zeal with which he gave his mind to the new undertaking was a novel experience in his existence. At Bygate he had never felt the stimulus of responsibility, and so his part in the affairs of the farm was purely mechanical, or rather a matter of diversion. He had there given all his enthusiasm to his books, and the transcendental imaginings arising out of them. He had never been a dreamer only, paralysed by metaphysical speculation. He was not highly developed enough for that. His pastoral employment, too, harmonised in his imagination with the tenor of his thoughts, so that no irksome antagonism was aroused. Had his temperament been in contact with industrial conditions from the outset, he would no doubt have drifted into some of the ordinary intellectual or imaginative courses, or have cumbered the earth uselessly.

It was therefore with a definite sense of depression that he returned to the town in the evening. The place was now so completely and exclusively associated with his personal anxieties and humiliations that it could no longer inspire in him any generous aim. This was rapidly combining with his deep-rooted peasant predilections to form a hatred of highly civilised life, and to find in it. only such issues as those which had overwhelmed himself. His intellectual, and we might almost say poetical, aptitude enabled him to invest this purely individual whim with all the vigour of first principles, and in his grim meditations to make it uncommonly bad for the civilised world.

It chanced that he had fallen into this censorious vein of reflection as he walked up to-night from the station, so that he reached home in anything but an amiable mood.   As he entered the door, his wife's engagement recurred to him.   " Not back yet, I'll warrant," he mused, in an unconvinced perverse manner ; but as he went into the room he found that his ill-humoured conjecture was perfectly true. Adelina was not there.   He rang for his tea.   No, Mrs. Crozier had not been back since the morning. So Sibbald devoured his tea in no better temper. He had brought in a paper with him, and as he ate he read, if only as a distraction.   Afterwards he read in the armchair, and continued reading until long after he could see no more.

They were long evenings, so he had not to light the gas early ; yet when he did light it, still Lina had not returned.   He flung away the paper and took a book.   This time he really did read, and got interested, so he looked up with positive amazement to find it eleven o'clock.   He walked about the room a little, then sat down again.   As the clock struck twelve he went to bed.

In the morning came no explanation, and he stayed in till noon. Anxiety was scarcely the word to express his feelings, for he was only too well assured that his wife could take care of herself. But at noon the ridiculous thought occurred to him, what if she does not come back at all? At first a sensation of terror came with the idea, but this rapidly passed to a dull weight of listless resignation. Such things *did* happen. In *these* places no doubt commonly enough. Then he got up and went out.

. Not twenty yards from the door he met Adelina returning on foot. His face showed actual surprise at seeing her, such root had that momentary thought taken. But seeing her colour he softened.

"Will you come into the Park?" he said. "Or perhaps you are hungry?"

"Yes, yes, I'll go," replied Adelina in a strange way for her, suggesting nervousness, which was not her predominant characteristic. "I'm not hungry."

She was indeed only too thankful to face it in the open air.

"I've been with Leila," said Lina with some unnecessary emphasis as they walked on.

"Yes," was all the reply, and there was nothing more until they had entered the Park gates.

"Of course, Lina, you must see that we can't possibly go on like this," began Sibbald, with some trace of renewed emotion, for his sensitive nature was too deep to withstand the personal contact.

"No, no, we can't," returned she with feverish excitement, her face excessively flushed, if he had been able to look at it. "Listen and I'll tell you all about it. Yesterday we went to Warkworth, and—and we went out to Coquet Island, and the two boatmen got tipsy, so that we couldn't get back until it was too late."

There was such a mixture of impulse and hesitation in her announcement that Sibbald felt an irresistible impression that it was false, that the whole thing was a fabrication, and the suspicion horrified him beyond endurance. His whole soul recoiled from such transactions, and between man and wife!

"Was he there?" demanded he after a moment's silence, the tone in which he spoke revealing something of what had passed within him during the interval. The circumstances involved such high tragedy that Adelina simply lied.

"No, he wasn't there."

He did not dare to turn and face her. Nay, his reverence for the exterior woman in her absolutely forbade it. But he saw none the less distinctly that hideous skeleton—those eyes haunted him. And as if to emphasise the contrast, suddenly and quite involuntarily the other, the ideal features, radiant with a heavenly light, started up before him.

At first they exercised so powerful and instantaneous an effect upon him that he shrank trembling, with all his faculties benumbed. He could not speak, could hear nothing of Lina's vehement asseverations about him, could see nothing of the common day, until, regardless, nay, ignorant, that she was still speaking, his tongue broke into a passionate appeal.

"Can't you see it? Can't you see the hideous life we are living? That we are not living a life at all; that we are writhing in the agonies of a horrible death? Only think of what marriage, of what home, of what a woman is! A very ray of the sun set by God in heaven to deliver us from everlasting night. And what have we made it? What have we made *her?*"

The outburst startled Lina, and instantly silenced her. He paused, and she was trembling for what should next come.

"And it is all *that* that has done it," continued Sibbald undauntedly, pointing to the smoke-cloud overhanging the town. "With that stretched above us how can we know that there is a God, that there is a sun, or that there is a heaven at all to live under ? If we had never come here we should never have got like those that live here. Our life would never have been broken; its light would never have been put out. Lina, my wife, my darling wife, come away, and let us save ourselves ! Let us seek the light again from which only we can get a ray of life. Far away you will feel the horror of this. Your woman's soul will come back to you, and all the tender love and happiness which *is* a woman will shine on us once more."

Mere stress of emotion brought the Scholar's voice to an end. He could not express what was in his soul ; its fulness choked him. He knew that he had spoken, but it seemed nothing of what he wished. When, however, he ventured to glance at his companion, he saw that tears were streaming down her cheeks. So they walked on for some minutes in silence, until, thinking Lina about to speak, Sibbald turned again to her.

" Let me—" she began faintly, but stopped, and he caught her in his arms to save her from falling.

There was a seat at hand, and upon it Crozier placed his wife. At sight of the apparently lifeless figure all the associations of a similar scene elsewhere rushed over him, and with them a flood of renewed tenderness for the girl. They had only seen some children since entering, and they were far away, so Sibbald was able to pay the necessary attentions without interruption. Water was not at hand, but it was soon apparent that this would not be necessary. At the first sign of her reviving he showered profuse caresses upon her, but to his dismay she pushed him off, not harshly or impatiently, but with a deliberate intention which he could not resist. She regained her breath heavily, whilst Sibbald's eyes were riveted anxiously upon her. After one glance, and seeing him there, Lina kept her own fast shut.

" Don't speak to me any more," she said presently in a tremulous voice. " I can't stand it."

Sibbald obeyed, and simply sat watching her. When she was sufficiently recovered they walked slowly home.

For the next day or two Crozier expected his wife to be seriously ill, and he stayed at home accordingly. She kept to her bed, and he used every form of entreaty to get her consent to his fetching a doctor, but this she vehemently forbade. She got excited about it, and declared that if a doctor came into the room she should jump out of the window. Seeing that the suggestion so deeply disturbed her, Sibbald allowed her to have her way, but he kept a very vigilant outlook upon her, at such times, that is, that she would allow him in the room. His offer to sit and read to her caused her even more disquiet than his desire for medical aid. She constantly declared that she was all right, and that she only wanted to be quiet. So he was obliged to acquiesce, and Adelina lay in her bed in solitary reflection.

She was unnaturally pale still, and her eyes were very red, although Sibbald had not seen her weep since those tears in the Park. Through those lonely hours she kept her eyes fixed upon the foot of the bed almost the whole time immovably, whilst her fingers played with the sheet and blanket. The whole aspect and behaviour seemed foreign to Lina, who was always either all vivacity or caprice. If she was not, indeed, reflecting, pondering some very critical juncture in her own or somebody else's affairs, she had a very remarkable faculty for simulating the attitude.

That startling and unforeseen reversal by Sibbald of all his past behaviour had momentarily overthrown Lina. She came back quite prepared for open displeasure or sullen reticence, and either of these would have sufficiently ministered to the frame of mind which it was absolutely necessary for her to sustain. It has been said before that Adelina, despite vast frivolity, was not utterly devoid of human sensibility. By so unexpectedly penetrating to her little fund of it, her husband had thrown her into a welter of contending inclinations such as he could little suspect in her, and of which she was as little equipped to be the subject. It was another case of that imperative necessity for Lina to make an independent decision, and it must have been the magnitude of the depending issue which overawed her even to the verge of a critical illness.

Thus things remained until Saturday morning. As he dressed, Sibbald had been unable to get a single word from Lina beyond the fact that she was better. "Much better," she had said. So he went down to his solitary breakfast. Whilst eating it with what appetite he had, he was rather surprised to see a policeman come up to the door. It was one of those events sufficiently unusual to excite a passing speculation without any personal interest in the

result. However, after he had rung and the summons had been answered, the servant came in to
Sibbald with a blank, if not exactly scared, expression of features, to say that there was a policeman to
see *him.* This touched Crozier's sense of humour,
although he felt a thrill of uneasiness himself.

" Well, ask him to come in. He doesn't want to
arrest me." So the policeman came in.

He was a civil young fellow, and exchanged greet-
ings rationally. He took the chair which Sibbald
indicated, as it was obvious he had something to
discuss. The only thought which passed through
Crozier's mind was that his father had been engaged
in some excess or brawl.

" You are the son of Mr. Crozier, sir, that lives at
No. 4 Murray Place ? "

" I am. Is he—? "

Sibbald meant to say " locked up," but an overwhelming shame checked him, and the other interposed.

" He's had some sort of a stroke, sir, and the doctor is in doubt whether he'll recover. I was called to No. 4 this morning by a neighbour, and certain representations were made to me. Nobody had been about for a day or two; they'd heard groaning the day before, and the like o' that. So I informed the inspector, and we broke open the door. We found the old gentleman unconscious on the floor, where it was thought he must have been some time. We got a doctor immediately, and he has since come round. He gave us your address, and perhaps you'll go along. He seems to have nobody with him in the house."

"No; he's been living in a queer way for some time," said Sibbald. " I'll go to him immediately. Will you have anything ? "

"Thank you, sir." And Crozier placed whisky and a tumbler before him, and rang for some water.

As the officer stated that he should have to go down there again, Sibbald volunteered to accompany him, and left the room to get ready. He gave the facts hurriedly to Adelina, who stared at him in silent wonder. Although obviously in haste, after telling her he stood at the foot of the bed irresolutely.

" You're sure you'll be all right ? "

Oh, yes, she felt much better. He must go at once.

" You really won't see a doctor ? "

" There's no need ; I'm well now." And she glanced furtively at him.

" Of course I don't know how long I shall be away. . . . I may have to stay all day. But I shall see. . . . I shall have to get him a proper nurse, and then I can run up to see— But good-bye ! "

With an impulsive movement Sibbald stepped to her side, and folded her tightly in his arms before she could offer any resistance.

" Good-bye, dearest," he said, kissing her ardently. Lina moved uneasily under his embrace, and gave no reply. One more tender glance he cast as he passed through the doorway, and then it was closed. Her eyes remained fixed there for some minutes after he had gone, then as she heard the street door open and shut, she buried her face in the pillow and burst into uncontrollable sobs.

Sibbald accompanied the policeman to his father's house. The old man was in bed, and the doctor was still sitting beside him.

" Here we are! " said the latter, rising as the young man entered. " Rather a bad job this."

Although evidently addressing the new-comer, the gentleman kept his eyes fixed upon the invalid, as if to note how he received the visitor. Then he nodded approvingly, and muttered, " That'll do, that'll do."

"Yes, yes, come on," he added in a louder tone. " He knows you. We shall pull him through all right."

Sibbald had also seen from the first glance his father gave him that he recognised him, and without

impatience, although he did not speak.   Judging
from the appearance of the old features, ten years
might have passed since last father and son met
instead of less than a week.   A hale, choleric man of
about sixty had altered to a decrepit figure on the
verge of the grave.   The shock to Sibbald was a
violent one, for the face so familiar to him seemed
radically altered, although he knew it to be the same.
It was impossible to associate with this object the
vehement characteristics which had played so essential a part in all Sibbald's life.   He himself seemed
to have aged ten years also in the reversed position
which this change in his father thrust upon him.
Yet did his sense of strength and superiority over-
whelm him with an agony of sympathy and commiseration.   He, and perhaps he only, could estimate
what a fall was there.   Having been already for
some days in a highly nervous condition, he found it
impossible altogether to repress his emotion, and as
the tears fell from his eyelashes, he turned away.

The doctor took the opportunity of a hurried consultation with him.

Although with the doctor's assistance an efficient nurse was immediately obtained, still Sibbald found plenty to engage him for the rest of the morning. He had left Lina much better; he had been able to observe it himself; therefore it was clear that his presence was very much more important here than there. The doctor had been anxious to discover something of the antecedent circumstances which had led to the catastrophe, but, except by way of general outline of his affairs, Sibbald was, of course, unable to satisfy him. His last interview with his father was, as he admitted, more or less of a violent kind, at least upon one side, but then that occurred on Tuesday. It then occurred to Sibbald that if anybody could know anything about it, it must be Daniel Curle. Therefore, when everything was in order, that is, about by mid-day, he resolved to set off and see Daniel. He went first to the office where the latter had been employed, and received the same information that his father had done. This surprised him. To the club; to Curle's lodgings. More and more surprising still. Nowhere was the man to be found; nor this only, for all the answers he had received seemed to suggest some amount of mystery.

At the lodgings the woman recognised Sibbald as having visited Curle, so she expanded even more fully than to the old man. In fact, she concluded with a reference to this latter incident in a manner which appeared to Crozier a clue.

" I've had others before you wanting him," she said as he was going out, and as if delighting in the innuendo she was able to append to the remark. " But none like an old man as came on Tuesday night. My! wasn't he mad? He was an impudent old wretch, and I don't know as I should be sorry to hear as Curle had done him out of a thousand pounds. It couldn't have been less, for you should have seen the sweat pouring down him as he read this letter, and *I* thought it was rather a cold night for the time of year. Do you think it *is* anything for the police?"

"Oh, no, nothing of that sort," said Sibbald hurriedly, as he took his leave. But in his own mind he was by no means assured of it.

It was evident, therefore, to young Crozier's comprehension that his father never had seen Curle since that mysterious appointment on Tuesday evening. Vague enough though his deductions, they were of a very unpleasant quality, and such as at anyrate to give some theoretical explanation of the shock his father had sustained. One other step suggested itself whilst he was on the inquiry, and that was an interview with Mr. Elliott. He would at least know if the purchase money had been paid, and when and by whom the matter had been completed. He set off with the resolute intention of investigating this, but on the way he paused, and ultimately abandoned the idea altogether.

His Crozier instinct came opportunely to rescue him from this extreme measure. If there were anything in his suspicions, a visit to Mr. Elliott could only impart a share of them to him also, and his father's affairs would inevitably become known. This, he could well suspect, would be anything but agreeable to his father, and if violently otherwise might very easily aggravate his disorder. Whatever then was the explanation of the mystery, Sibbald concluded that his own part must be one of complete ignorance as directly affecting his father, and to this he adhered. As he was in the town, he had his dinner there, and went afterwards to Murray Place.

The nurse was downstairs when he arrived, and expressed satisfaction that he had come. His father, she said, had asked for him, and had shown some little annoyance that he was not there. Just then the old man's bell rang, and the nurse ran upstairs. Sibbald stood at the foot of them, and from the top in a minute or two she beckoned him up.

As he entered the room, the youth was at once unpleasantly aware of his father's eyes. All the room seemed but as a frame for them, and their only object a burning scrutiny of himself. They followed him as he moved, and seemed intent upon extracting some information from him.

"Shut the door!" said the invalid in all the voice that remained to him, and Sibbald obeyed, as he also did the sign for him to be seated.

The chair had been placed by the side of the foot of the bed, so that the old man from his pillow could command the full features of anybody occupying it. For two whole minutes now in silence had the Scholar to undergo the fevered gaze of those eyes. He himself dared not break the silence nor move a muscle of his face, either of which actions on his part, he was well aware, would have put the meeting to an end. At length his patience was rewarded.

"I'm dean," said the old man, in a tone which itself announced the collapse of a character.

"Ay," said the other, bowing his head, mingling just the necessary proportions of acquiescence and sympathy.

"Daniel Curle has robbed me of three thousand pounds—a' that I got for By—but that's no het." He paused and looked nervously around him, as if he was suspicious of being overheard. Then again his eyes rested on his son, and silence fell.

"But what's the gear?" he next added, with almost a flash of spirit. "Juist naething at a'; that's no het."

The struggle that was going on within was painfully apparent. But Sibbald thought it spiritual rather than physical. The old fellow seemed unable to compel himself to make the statement which he knew must come, and for which alone he had demanded his son's presence. What confession he could have to make of such tragical import the youth could not, dared not, surmise. . . . Had he murdered Curle? . . , It was that hideous and involuntary thought which had so suddenly blanched Sibbald's features and quivered through his whole frame.

" I hae wranged ye—listen, man, and ye'll ken why the noo—ay, I hae wranged ye. Bygate was no mine to sell."

This relieved Sibbald, for it proved conclusively that his father was rambling. He knew only too well to the contrary—moreover, had not Mr. Elliott accepted the title ? The youth's colour returned, and he could listen with some measure of sympathetic calm.

" It was no mine to sell. . . . It aye belanged to the Croziers. I sellt it because *ye* werena yane. . . . Ay ! . . . Because *ye* poisoned the breed. Oh, man, I hae wranged you sair."

" But I have poisoned it, father," exclaimed Sibbald warmly, if only to calm the old man, from whose eyes he felt bound to flee.

" I'm no denying that, man. . . . Bygate was aye the property o' the Croziers. But—but ye hae only

poisoned it mair. It was yours as muckle as my ain
—for—for I'm no yane o' them mysel', ye ken."

He spoke the last words slowly, and with an awful
solemnity of emphasis, as though the whole round
world fell with the confession.

" I'm no better nor ye," he went on. " Nay, I'm
waur, I'm waur, for I was aa'd enough to hae kent it
before."

Then he relapsed into silence, and fixed those eyes
once more upon his son.

" Then if we are as bad as each other, there's no
need for us to quarrel any more," said Sibbald, looking up.

" But I'm waur, I'm waur. Ye had a woman to
get, of a kind, but I lost a'. I'm far waur, I tell ye.
I hae robbed ye tae, man. . . . But I'm gaun,
Sib."

" You think I had better start a quarrel with you
then ? " demanded the son in a lighter vein than he
had felt for many a day. " We'll put that off a bit.

I'm tired of quarrels, and I'd rather wait for another opportunity."

The old man stared at him in some bewilderment, it is just possible not without a strong suspicion of contempt.

" And—and ye'll gan for the police, daur say ? " he said, again in quavering tones, and this time without any disguise of his suspicion.

" Certainly not," was the emphatic reply, for he had already faced this contingency when he turned back from going to Mr. Elliott. "It is no concern of mine. I shall not say a word to anybody about it. . . . Certainly not to my wife."

The old features grew distinctly easier. For this he had not dared to hope. Sibbald watched the old man fall back on the pillow with a huge sigh of relief, and at length the eyes were removed, even the eyelids closed.

Without any remark the youth got up. At the door he looked back, and saw the eyes give a parting glance at him, but there was no movement of recall. So he went out of the room.

Very soon after this Sibbald was on his way home. Such a state of lightheartedness was new to him, so unfamiliar that he hardly expected it to last. His heart none the less was vociferating jubilant thanks to Curle for his villainy. Nothing short of it, he was sure, could have rendered such effectual assistance ; nothing less have rescued the old man from an ignoble, a revolting doom. Even a spice of jocularity entered into his reflections on his father's position, tragical though it was. The sincerity of the farmer's reasoning was undoubted. Unquestionably he did consider himself as degraded for ever from the ranks of his ancient race, and that therefore his life in any aggressive sense was ended.

As he approached his own abode Sibbald's thoughts were changed. They reverted to that very different figure he had left so abruptly in the morning, and a tremulous expectancy rose up in him at the prospect of the meeting. The solemn vehemence of that appeal to which his emotions had once again urged him had, in cooler blood, suffered considerable eclipse, but it had left permanent good to him by recording on his soul an aim to which he knew his most exalted moments would aspire. It would serve as an aid and stimulus to himself when the common day should obscure the transcendent within him, and to it he would desperately cling. With such high and loyal purpose he went in.

Lina was not in the sitting-room, so he ran lightly upstairs. She was not there; the bed was made. He stood for a moment to wonder before again descending.

CHAPTER V.

THE REMNANTS.

IT seemed strange to him that if she had felt well enough for a walk she should choose this particular time for it, but, of course, so it might be. He himself was weary with the doings of the day, so he threw himself upon the sofa to collect his thoughts as to the general progress of affairs. His mind had scarcely got to Whaupriggs before there was a knock at the outer door, which he knew for the postman. But he never received letters, so it did not concern him. This afternoon, however, one was brought in for him.

When the girl had withdrawn, he rose up to examine the envelope standing. He had already stared at it with parted lips from every possible point of view, but alteration of his own position might afford yet one more. The post-mark was Newcastle-on-Tyne only; the hand-writing was—Adelina's. Into such a tremulous state of agitation did this mere survey plunge him that he was incapable of opening it. His whole soul rose in a paroxysm of terror, and, like a woman, he felt that he must burst into a flood of tears, to such a pitch had the nervous tension of recent days worked him. This he was spared, however, and instead, he flung the letter on the table and walked to and fro across the room.

When at length he tore it open, all the words the letter contained were these—"*It is too late.*" No beginning, no signature. The writing was his wife's, but written unsteadily, and on the last *o* of the *too* the pen had caught in the paper and spurted.

"It is too late." The words rang through his brain like the knell of the highest aspiration of his existence. It was impossible for him to misunderstand them. Words like these, and in such a way, were not written upon an ordinary occasion—upon setting off for a day's picnic in the country for instance.   They had some deeply tragical import, and Sibbald's frame quivered, the perspiration stood on his brow, and he inevitably concluded what it was.   The picture of the pair arriving in the station that day, and which had so appalled him, was at once presented.   But it all seemed to have come upon him with such overwhelming suddenness. The horror of it was inconceivable.   Whatever their little differences,—and he admitted his own disillusionment,—*this* catastrophe could by no possibility have been prepared for in his mind.   But for that vision of the station, he could not now have dreamed of it.   Any other explanation would have been easy, inevitable.   A discontented woman might impulsively fly from her husband—take refuge under the roof of a friend, just as it were to get outside her position ; to see from neutral ground of what her discontent existed, to consider how it might be re-

moved. But something with devouring flames assured him that with Adelina it would not be so.
Something unspeakable, something irrevocable, he
knew, *must* accompany such action in her. Not because of the evil that was in her, but just because
there was nothing in her at all. Had she proved a
strong, evil woman (if in his thought such a creature
could exist in nature), his agony would not have been
one half so intolerable. It was her very feebleness
that extorted such a cry of anguish from him, that at
length plunged him into such a welter of remorse.
He must have contributed to the catastrophe. Nay,
he knew he had. His chivalrous soul, yearning ever
towards the protection of a woman, could now arraign
him of every possible crime. If he were so much the
stronger, ought not his patience to have been so much
the more supreme? Every smallest paroxysm of impatience rose to thrust its sting into his soul. " It is
too late."

After the first stupefying effect of the announcement, Sibbald awoke to the fact that something must be done, if for no other reason than that he could not be still. To stay here and nurse his calamity would drive him mad. To rush aimlessly abroad would just as surely effect it. What—what in heaven's name could he do?

Suddenly the name of Leila Featherstone came into his mind. He had never seen the girl; he vehemently loathed her; but to her he would go. He did not know where she resided, but he could go to every Featherstone in the town and demand if such a daughter was theirs. So on this errand he set off. He went first to the public library, and from the Directory copied the address of every Featherstone he could find. He only obtained four.

At the very first house he applied to he was informed that Miss Leila Featherstone was at home. In he went, and sent in his name, for cards he had none. In a minute or two a young lady appeared, and instinct at once assured him he was right.

"I hope you will forgive me calling," he began with politeness, but ingenuous impetuosity. "I am the husband of your friend Adelina Brett, and I wish to ask if you can tell me where she is."

"It is more than a week since I have seen her," said the other in a nervous tone of astonishment, and all colour going out of her face.

"More than a week! But you were with her at Warkworth on Wednesday?"

The girl shook her head, and Sibbald felt an un-expected thrill of confidence in her. He saw, at least, that she would not tell him a lie. Great terror was depicted upon her face.

"You were not!" And Sibbald turned under another stab. "Oh, tell me anything you know!" exclaimed he with unrestrained fervour. "I must find her to-day."

"B-but, I'm sure I don't know anything at all."

"But you suspect something. Tell me what you think."

"I can't!" declared the girl, turning hurriedly away to leave the room he feared, but he stepped forward.

"I implore you to help me," continued Sibbald with pathetic earnestness of appeal. "She has left home, and I feel that she does not intend to return to me. Tell me—do tell me where you think she has gone!"

The girl still had her back towards him in another part of the room. She was thinking how handsome Sibbald was, and burning with shame at the pictures she had drawn of him. She did not dare to speak.

"I assure you it is horrible to me to have to distress you, but there is nobody else I can ask, and—and the whole of her life is at stake. I must—must find her. . . . Do you think she has gone with him?" he added in a lower tone, for he could restrain himself no longer.

"I am afraid—" she faltered without moving in the least,

"With Robson ? "

The name was poison on his tongue, but he dared not risk an uncertainty. She nodded.

"Then please give me his address, and I will trouble you no longer."

She did so, and he wrote it down, for he could not trust to his memory. Then he moved as if to go.

"Again I beg you to forgive me for coming here. I could think of no other way. Under *such* circumstances you will forgive me."

"I—I am so sorry for you," said Leila in a broken voice. "I—I told her. It is wicked—wicked of her."

Sibbald looked in astonishment, and saw that she was weeping. The touch of human sympathy, and from a woman, did him good, and he left the house in a different mood.

The address she had given him was not very far off, so he walked directly thither. Mr. Charles Robson was not at home. Could they possibly tell him where he had gone to? It was of the utmost importance that he should see him. Inquiry was made, and with the answer whirling through his brain, Sibbald shrank away, knowing that he was defeated. Mr. Robson had left for Paris that morning.

For a few days Sibbald himself was in danger of being ill, but his constitution withstood it. He had made no further inquiry, and no other word of explanation arrived. His father, who was pronounced to be progressing favourably, did not wish him much about him, so by the middle of the week he went to Whaupriggs, and lodged at an adjoining cottage until he could get his plans a little more distinct.

He stayed there a week, going about his occupations as though he had been established at the farm. The definite employment and the moorland air allayed his agitation and confirmed him in a philosophic calm. The burning horror of that broken life elsewhere, partly also his own, could not soon be dimmed in him, but he gained a fuller ability of allowing it less exclusive play, of thrusting this practical work into the very forepart of his brain. He had engaged such people as he wanted for the farm, including upon this last occasion a woman from Crawston well known to him who was to undertake all the inner affairs of his house. His only concern now was the furniture, and he returned to the town with meditations also about that.

The resignation of his father had in that momentous interview been unconditional, so at least Sibbald had thought, and upon it he now felt warranted to some extent in building. Every farthing of his outlay had he rigidly to calculate, and if, by utilising what of the Bygate furniture his father had saved, a hundred pounds could be rescued, it made his position by that much the sounder. He came back, therefore, with the intention of surveying his father's ground.

Of the old man's health he received reassuring accounts. Of recovery there was now no sort of question. The only doubt in the medical mind was how great a degree of incapacity would permanently remain with him. His mind varied greatly. Some days he could converse with perhaps an exceptional amount of rationality; others he muttered in every appearance of unreason. Happily, this day of Sibbald's arrival was, he was told, one of the good ones; one of the best for several days past. When he was told of his son's visit, the invalid expressed immediately a readiness to see him. So Sibbald went up.

That he thrust out his hand, although it was the left one (of the right he had not the use), was an unusually favourable sign, as Sibbald instantly construed it. The old man then pointed to the chair, and his visitor saw with considerable relief that the eyes had lost that terrible fixity which had agitated him before. He himself thought he was assuming a particularly severe expression, until his father's first remark undeceived him.

" What's wrang wi' ye?" demanded the latter in surprise.

The exclamation came so abruptly that Sibbald also was astonished. But he disclaimed the knowledge of anything being wrong. The other frowned, and seemed about to get angry. So the youth considered the opportunity had come, and he seized it.

" I've had a lot to do at Whaupriggs, and it has bothered me. I have had to find a housekeeper."

" What does a married man want with a housekeeper?" returned his father still in a severe tone and eyeing him askance.

" My wife doesn't like living in the country, and— and she has left me."

The announcement seemed to puzzle the old man at first, and he had the appearance of trying to connect it logically in his mind. Then came a flash of enlightenment.

" Then *ye* hae lost an' a'!" cried he almost jubilantly, an expression which Sibbald could only connect with the reference to family characteristics in their former conversation.

"I have lost an' a'," assented he quietly.

This revelation still exercised such an unexpected and powerful effect upon old Crozier, that he was kept silent, and his eyes played with uncomfortable pertinacity about his son's face. The latter was anxious for his own immediate relief, as well as for the furtherance of his project, to advance to his next point, but he had constantly in his mind the necessity of the most wary procedure, so he restrained himself.

"Left ye," muttered the old man at last. "But will ye no fetch her back?" There was a conscious-ness of his own degeneracy in the diffidence with which he put the question.

"Certainly not. If a woman won't live with me willingly, I shall never try to make her."

"No, no, lad, ye're right there. Ay, ay, ye're right enough there. Well, did ye hear the like o' that!"

And again the old fellow was lost in the depths of wonderment.

"And it seemed to me," Sibbald went on calmly and naturally, "that as we are both now alone, and both done, we might as well live together at Whaup-riggs. Your advice would help me a good deal with the stock, and although I'm not a Crozier, I might be a bit of company—"

"But I'm no yane mysel'," interposed the other in a deep voice. "I tellt ye sae."

"Then we should be on the same ground. We shouldn't quarrel or annoy each other."

"Daur say no."

Sibbald observed that his suggestion was working, so he was prudent enough to let it take its own course a while, and he sat silent. In a minute or two the result was apparent. The eyes became restless; the lips seemed about to speak. At length it came.

"Man, I'll gan wi' you."

After coming to this unconditional agreement,

Sibbald went more fully into the subject of his farm. He gave full particulars of the extent and nature of it. Described the house—

" Bless ye, man, I ken it nicely," the old man put in with a laugh, the first laugh registered for a considerable time. So Sibbald went on to the number and quality of the sheep he had bought, the various other preparations he had made, all of which received the unqualified approval of the experienced farmer.

" Ye might hae put in a few mair hoggs for the hinder end, ye ken ; but they'll dea, man ; they'll dea."

As with himself, Sibbald saw distinctly that the mere discussion of such topics touched an inextinguishable vein in his father, and recalled with it a new measure of vitality. So when he considered he had stayed long enough, he left with a substantial improvement in his spirits, and readily gave a promise to come again.

Thus, then, were these delicate questions adjusted

between father and son, and the end of another week saw them making active preparations for their final departure from the town. Things being so arranged, the doctor thought it highly probable that the moor-land air might now be highly beneficial to the further recovery of his patient, who, he admitted, had made remarkable strides for a man of his years. It was decided, therefore, that they should go forthwith, and should take the nurse with them until it was clear how things were to proceed. Although giving such a hopeful general account, the doctor thought it his duty to have a few confidential words with Sibbald as to the other side of the case.

"Of course, in these cases," said he, "there is no kind of certainty. There may be improvement one day, and—death the next. Happily, Mr. Crozier's constitution is an unusually robust one. Absolutely well he can never be, but it is highly probable that he will, in time, be able to walk with the assistance of sticks. He may live for ten years; another seizure, and he may die to-morrow. You see exactly how it is. There certainly is one ugly symptom in this case. The brain has been undoubtedly affected. I should esteem it a favour if you would keep me informed as to the progress of this, just in a friendly way, of course. I am very much interested in the case. It is unnecessary to tell you to keep, so far as possible, out of his way any source of agitation. That is the principal thing to observe. Violent agitation would kill him at any time."

It was with almost childish excitement that Sibbald commenced the dismantling of that house. Despite all the far from childlike elements that had crept into his life of late, these were just now over-ridden by the wild zeal with which he turned his eyes to the silence of the hills. It was like a boy packing up at school. Here alone, dungeons and chains; there the open expanse of heaven, the deliverance from every galling thing.

The old man stood the journey well, in spite of

his disabled condition. As he drove the necessary miles from the last station, an impenetrable silence settled on him, but by furtive glances his son saw the glitter in his eyes as they travelled over the summer prospect. It was hot, and massive thunder-clouds were rolling over the mountains, imparting to them their most characteristic aspect of solemn, frowning majesty. A cloudless, smiling day would probably have made the farmer irritable from lack of sympathy with the lowering profundity of his own reflections. The effect upon him was in strong contrast to that which was felt by Sibbald: all the contrast existing between a November and an April storm. Winter and night sit behind the one; spring and high noonday.lurk in the fringes of the other. But even Sibbald *was* in storm.

The house was not so large as Bygate, but still a substantial stone-built place, showing the repairs of recent years. A few trees were scattered round it to the north and west, and a steep green hill rose

immediately behind, with some grey crags jutting
out, beside which grew tall bracken, some foxgloves
rising in pink bud, and a few stunted birch trees.
In front, a crease went down to the Rede water,
filled with alders in the lower part, and the house
commanded an unbroken prospect of the main
valley east and west.

As they ascended the open track after leaving the
road, Sibbald noticed that his father frequently
shook his head ominously, even muttered occasionally ; the son, as he thought, catching once the word
"clarty," sinister word to the Border farmer's ear.
But he took no notice, affected not to hear. When
they came at length beside the house, the elder
stared aggressively around, and Sibbald feared, but
only for an instant.

"Ah, weel, I hae seen a waur place," exclaimed
the old man loudly. "Just twa-three here and there,
ye ken." And Sibbald was more than content.

A week or two seemed to promise unexpected

success to the venture, at any rate from a spiritual point of view. High summer was just upon them and it was a beautiful one, affording conditions soothing to the spirits of all. Old Crozier violently refused the comforts of a bath-chair which Sibbald obtained for him, persistently reviling it as the perambulator, and accusing them all of intending the most flagrant insult against him, by thus trying to turn him into a bairn.

"A Crozier of sixty-three—" But there came a tragic pause, and Sibbald strode away, leaving the old man to smother his own confusion as he' best might.

He just had his own Bygate arm-chair carried into such place as he selected, and there he would sit by the hour, apparently contemplating the scene around him. No doubt he did not contemplate it at all, but there was nothing to show that he contemplated anything else.

Although he maintained a consistent outward composure and engaged zealously in all the work of his farm, upon Sibbald, no doubt, fell the principal share of the suffering. To some measure of philosophy a vigorous soul may attain, but there are moments, nay, hours and days, when all the armour is rent and nothing may staunch the bleeding of the wounds. Sibbald knew such days, and then the burden of his woe would appear insupportable. To one of his ardent, exalted temperament, the shattering in a few months of what appeared the only sustaining idea for a whole life was no trivial infliction. Nay, the very centre of the calamity was that the idea was by no means shattered; it was only the preliminary application of it that had fallen. From the ashes the vital heat still glowed with redoubled intensity and brilliance. So much had been burned away that only now was the genuine glow discernible at all. Woe, woe unutterable!

He trusted to time to aid him, but it seemed to have exactly the opposite effect. As active weeks sped on into months and he saw the crimson of the distant hills turning into brown, he knew that the anguish, the yearning of his soul, was more acute, less resistible, than when first it had burst upon him.

The only modification of it was that also more of the
sympathetic was blended with it. If his own agony
was intensified, so was his emotion on behalf of
that other that had caused it. Time at least was
weaving around *her* a halo of pure pathos. The in-
significant motes in the common day were rapidly
subsiding, and when he dared to call up the image of
her, or rather when he was utterly unable to escape
it, he could only see a beautiful image of etherealised
suffering, with the tearful shame-stricken eyes ap-
pealing with awful silence to *him*. If he had known
it, no doubt herein lay the stoutest bulwark of his
philosophy. Had he been able to harbour a single
reproach against her, immediately had chaos overwhelmed him. But now he could not. There was
nothing voluntary in the emotion. He had not to
strain his soul to shower commiseration, pardon upon
her. Such was the natural effluence of his being,
issuing every day in greater force the longer this
silence continued. Not pardon in the sense of con-
donation, for that dream was white in the ashes, but
unconditional forgiveness of all wrong, unconditional

shelter from the blasts and ice-floes of a heartless world, such as he felt must irresistibly assail her.

As the days of autumn advanced, from being a pure emotion, this instinct took shape before him. Sibbald felt that he ought to do something. None the less, from direct action he shrank with deepest shuddering. The only practical step which was presented he utterly refused to take, and that was to inquire into the movements of Robson. So still day after day passed on.

In spite of these growing agitations within, outward life at the farm proceeded as usual. From being confined more to the house, the old man developed greater irritability, but also with it increased physical power. He had long recovered the use of his arm, and by the time the Martinmas winds were blowing, with his son's assistance he could cross the room. But after the first trial he could not be got to make the attempt again. He got angry if it was suggested. Secretly, however, he tried his powers with the greatest pertinacity by shuffling persistently round the table, and he was himself astonished at the effect produced. The progress which he felt stimulated (certain confessions, notwithstanding) the Crozier within him, and by December he threatened to knock Sibbald down with a stick because he volunteered to get him something from the other side of the room. In astonishment, the young man saw him skirt the table and cross the strait between it and the wall, but dared make no remark, and had to accept it as a matter of course.

By the middle of December they had had a very deep fall of snow, and beyond the hand feeding of the sheep, all the work was at a standstill. By so rigorously restricting his activity, this very seriously increased Sibbald's annoyances. Never a day now passed without his contemplating that one project which was becoming fixed in his mind, and assuming there a more and more prominent position. His own powerlessness depressed him, and yet every day his passionate desire to do something grew stronger. One morning, in a desperate search for something to distract him, he shut himself up in his room, and began to open some of his boxes of books.

As he took out a once favourite volume, he would walk with it to the window, and stand there dipping into what now struck him as almost strange. It was with a shock of surprise that he found how his spirit had altered, and from the page he would cast a reflective glance outside. Even to him the prospect there was cheerless. All the landscape of unbroken white, save where the bed of the river ran, and where the hill-tops gave place to a sullen lead-coloured sky. Whilst he was so much confined, these glances became more frequent, and more prolonged. Perhaps the association of the books with the landscape recalled, with such peculiar force, similar scenes during the previous winter. He was rapidly travelling back exactly to what he had come here to escape. Every moment his agitation increased, and finally the books were flung aside altogether.

He now found himself battling with an impression which he was resolute not to entertain. With such mysterious abruptness, and such overwhelming vehemence had it assailed him, that he was the more fully persuaded of its evil source. It was the figure of Jenniper that had risen up before him with some subtle suggestions of assistance in its train. "Go to her," a thousand voices urged him, "and she will tell you what to do." But in the echo his conscience insisted upon hearing a jeer. He would not go to Jenniper, of that he was resolved. Even if action should lie in that direction, not through that direction should it be pursued. Jenniper Curle, save as a transfigured abstraction, he had seen for the last time; to that conclusion he had firmness to adhere. So he considered the tempter routed, and went out of the house.

The cold wind blowing over the snow braced up his nerves, and enabled him to smile defiance to all assaults. Since the indoor occupation had so miserably failed him, he decided to keep to the out, and went to the stable for his horse. He knew that the road below had been opened, and a scamper in the teeth of such a wind would finally blow away any lingering fog, if it could not impart the needed suggestion.

The horse's hoofs crunched the crisp snow as he walked down the slope. An afflicted bird would twitter past him, and on the air came the trouble of some distant sheep.

He took the road down the valley, in the direction of Horsley and Otterburn, setting off at a brisk trot, without looking much about him. Nobody else was abroad, and there were but few signs of life, except the clumps of sheep huddled in sheltered corners, with the snow trodden, and the hay spread about them. When he reached the church he slackened his pace, and straightened himself in the saddle to look round. There was some farmer's cart half a mile ahead, apparently coming in his direction, but no other movement. He went on.

In another minute a mysterious sensation of alarm and excitement possessed him. From having been staring before him, his eyes had fallen to his horse's ears, and not until some seconds had passed did he venture to raise them in a furtive glance. From alarm, his emotion quickly leapt to galloping joy, frantic, maddest abandonment to a delirious pleasure.

Was he not really out here in the snow? Was not the north wind blowing upon him assurance of tingling flesh? It was no dream; no vision such as those he *had* had, one scarce an hour ago. With heightened colour, instead of a furtive glance, he now again stared jubilantly before him. Nay, he raised his arm, and flourished it above his head. But a few seconds more he drew rein, and they drew rein, and there, immediately before him, was Jenniper Curle.

CHAPTER VI.

REFUGE.

JENNIFER and her father undoubtedly sat in that cart which he first so casually had noticed. Immediately he was beside them, all Sibbald's glee went out, and he merely received them with a cordial neighbourly greeting. There was nothing mirthful about them ; but in that there was nothing unusual. David Curle was not a man of mirth, and towards Crozier his daughter had never displayed hers.

"What on earth brings you travelling on sicna day ? " was Sibbald's first exclamation when he was able to speak.

"We were coming to Whaupriggs," replied the girl, who was evidently the mover in the expedition.

"Then it's the greatest mercy that I stopped you," returned he quickly, "for it would hae killed my

138

father to see you. He is tarr'ble bad, ye ken, and I
have to keep out of his way anything that puts him
in mind of Bygate. But I'm right glad to see you,"
he went on, with a smile ; "and we couldna ha' met
at a better part of the road. We'll just gan to the
' Arms,' and I can at least offer you some dinner."

The inn was close at hand, and without waiting for
an answer, Sibbald turned his horse and led the way.
He could not fail to perceive that even Jenniper was
more than usually solemn, and an irresistible conviction flashed on him that she must have come about
her. Utterly mad as the supposition would, in cool
blood, have seemed to him, it became now simply a
foregone thing. This put him into a state of nervous
agitation, and he spoke no more until they were
under shelter.

Sibbald gave up his horse to the man that
appeared, with instructions for both that and the
other, but Curle went round to the stable. After a
few further words with the landlady about dinner,
Crozier went into the room to Jenniper, whom he
found rubbing her hands before the fire. She jumped

up with alacrity at his step, and turned to face him.
The meeting of their eyes was enough.

"You have come to tell me about Adelina," said
he, in a low, eager tone.

She nodded.

"Let us go outside."

And the two went on to the frozen road, and
walked by the edge of the wood for some distance
before speaking a word.

"She is at Angryhaugh," announced the girl at
last, since he showed no sign of breaking the silence.
"She came the day before yesterday."

"Through the snow?" exclaimed Sibbald.

"She walked through the snow. Oh, I canna,
canna tell you what she came like. She takes a' the
blame," Jenniper proceeded, as her companion made
no attempt to speak. "She darena come to you
hersel', but she wants to know if you will see her just
once again. Oh, she's in sair trouble, poor lass."

Through his own excessive emotion, it still
occurred to Sibbald that Jenniper betrayed more
than was her wont.

"Jenniper, it has blighted my life for months. I have longed to find her, longed to do for her anything that a human being could do. See her? I shall, of course, fetch her home. Married again we can never be, but we can at least find some way of— of making her life different from this."

"I told her you would say that," asserted the other with unnecessary vehemence. "I knew you would."

"Why should she be afraid of me? . . . Oh, poor lass, poor lass!"

Both felt that they were in no condition to prolong such an interview, so they hurriedly proceeded to the necessary arrangements. Sibbald insisted upon returning with them that day, and himself talking over with the unhappy fugitive what could now be done. Now that the actual deed was upon him, he found all his sympathetic ardour maintained, all his vehement desires to shield her, at least from this December world, deepened. Perhaps associations of that figure once before in the snow intensified his tenderness, but if so, in a widely different way. It is doubtful if commonplace reproach had at any time arisen in his mind in connection with Lina's behaviour; now such was for ever an impossibility. Again they had ceased talking before they reached the inn.

Sibbald pretended to sit at the table with them; but they had scarcely begun ere he was up again, under the excuse of scribbling a message to his father. He had then to make arrangements for a messenger, this and that to do, so that the time of the meal slipped away, and his chair remained empty, his plate untouched. All his food was—to be off.

Curle again went round whilst the horses were being got ready. The other two were again alone.

" Where *is* my brother ? " asked Jenniper, with an abruptness which startled Sibbald out of the reverie into which he had fallen.

" My lass, I dinna ken," said he, looking frankly into her face. " I—I believe he has gone abroad."

" Do you ken why he left Newcastle so strangely?"

As it seemed with absolute composure, he withstood her gaze, then he said, without a quaver, " No." He added presently, " We could never get on together," and the subject was at an end.

They had more than two hours' ride over the hills to the Braid valley, with every mile of the journey Sibbald's agitation increasing. The scene was one of the most appalling desolation, and, after a trivial remark about the flocks, not a word was uttered all the way. The wind alone sighed most disconsolately over the snow-bound fells; but otherwise there was the silence of death all around them. A black line along the bottoms of the valleys, a black crag, wall-side or fir-clump on the slopes, a black, silently float-ing crow above them; no other variation to blank earth and sky.

" I'll just tell her you're here," said Jenniper, when she at length alighted, and went into the house.

With an extraordinary confusion of feeling, Sib-bald stood by his horse to cast his eye across the valley towards Bygate. There it was, backed by its belt of fir trees, as though *he* had never moved. This aspect was so familiar to him here, and was, strangely, without any melancholy suggestion. The place, under any aspect and any conditions, simply inspired him with the sensation of home. Since that com-

promise with Lord Braiddale, his continuity of existence here was hardly broken. He only lived to
return here, and at his age, with temperament such
as his, sanguine expectation partakes largely of
possession. Perhaps for a second his mind had been
able to travel over there; at least, when Jenniper
touched him, he looked round with a start.

" Dinna stay long the day."

" But—she must go back with me."

Jenniper simply shook her head in decided negative.

All had left the house save Adelina alone, who sat
in a chair by the fire. It was true that a few months
had sadly altered her. Her face was completely
without colour, and every feature was pinched, the
temple bones painfully suggesting extreme pressure
on the brain within. Her eyes only were brilliant
with an unnatural lustre, and showed no trace of
tears. Her withered lips now twitched with some
nervous uncertainty, and her fingers were not still,
but otherwise she presented a picture of utterly listless suffering, as though the picture, unspeakably

distressing to a beholder, did not exactly arise from any like intensity of feeling within. Hearing the step, she turned. "Oh, Sib—" she began, but was checked mostly by something in herself, but partly by her husband's solemn approach, for he had a hand raised as though to caution her from rising. Lina had not, in fact, intended to rise; very likely she did not feel the strength to do so.

One glance was enough for Sibbald, and it pierced his heart. His mind was so built upon ideals that he scarcely saw a hopelessly erring wife through the frail, the suffering, woman. She did not weep, but, after that glance, all to *him* floated in a haze before him. He walked up to her and placed his hand upon her hair. It was beautiful hair, but now all carelessly flung up, uncombed, unbrushed, evidently, for a long time. She raised her face to him vacantly, unemotionally, it might have seemed.

"I knew that you, at any rate, wouldn't let me die in the snow," she said.

"In the snow," echoed Sibbald faintly. But he could not repress himself, and muttering her name, he leaned down and folded her in his arms, with all the tenderness of a mother for her child. Then Lina burst into uncontrollable tears and sobs against his breast.

Sibbald rode back over that desolate waste alone when the early winter twilight was falling; but he saw nothing of the gloom. It could scarcely be joy that illumined him, at least not of the commonest kind. It was an ardent and brilliant emotion, certainly, and one which he had never experienced before. Love, such as he had known it, had been a selfish, tyrannical emotion, inciting him to vast enthusiasms, but imparting little, if any, placid joy. Therefore it was not renewed love that accompanied him. Unbounded placid *joy* was exactly what now he did feel at his wife's return. Not pleasure, mirth, gladness, jollity, but profound, subdued joy. He would tend her until she was well; he would provide for her peaceful life afterwards; all with such infinitude of joy as he had never before known.

He had to borrow a lantern on the way, so impenetrable fell the darkness, and yet he reached home before six. As he approached, one other difficulty confronted him. It was doubtful how his father might take this return. But that difficulty Sibbald faced promptly and fearlessly. If it was a case of life and death to him, equally so was it to her who was rescued, and she was a woman. One flitting thought of placing Adelina in other hands just arose, but was dispelled before it was fully formed. The idea was instinctively repugnant to him. That would not be restoring her to home; she could not feel that that was forgiveness. Under his own roof should she be tended, and, largely, by his own hand. What he had learned of her critical state of health rendered that imperative. Whatever was to be the result to her, Sibbald's first and central impulse was to surround her with the warmth of tenderness, to thaw and to expel the chill of isolation from her kind, which he imagined she must feel. Whatever her future life was to become, that must be instilled, must form part of the new breath she was taking at this critical time.

His father had shown a strange irritation at his absence, and was angry at his return. So Sibbald accepted the opportunity of settling the matter forthwith.

"Whar hae ye been, man?" roared he, as his son entered with a breath of the night air about him. "Do you want to be smoored in a snaw-wreath, that ye gan gadling aboot the hills on sicna day?"

It was merely that Sibbald's mysterious absence had suggested a surreptitious journey to Bygate in his mind, and the idea had kept him in a fever all day. The youth's appearance as he came in confirmed the notion, and so put light to the train.

"I have been to see my wife," was the calm reply, at which the other stared and kept his mouth open. "She is ill, and wants to come home."

"Well, my sartie, did ye ever hear the like o' that? And ye'll let her, I'se warr'nd," said his father in a biting manner.

"Certainly I shall. She is coming here to-morrow."

The authoritative yet calm tone in which the

announcement was made had a beneficial effect upon the old man, for although he continued to grumble and to growl at the remarkable doings of some folks, any active opposition was evidently far from his mind. His aggressive manner was immediately altered, and from time to time he would cast a stealthy glance at Sibbald, indicating anything but malevolence. The son observed more than he was credited with by the hazy old faculties, and he had for some time detected a growing submission to, almost awe of, himself, and subtle diffidence in opposing him, (although often disguised under the cloak of testiness to be sure), which gave some indication of the elder's perception of the superior power. This feeling was in reality very much deeper than Sibbald supposed, or than the old man's behaviour gave a notion of.

The following day accordingly Sibbald fetched his wife from Angryhaugh, and every preparation was made for her reception at Whaupriggs. A dazed submissive contentment marked Adelina through it all, but very little active participation in what went on. Towards Sibbald she displayed a

timid confidence of a purely animal nature. Her
strongest expression of approbation, thanks, or interest was, "Oh, Sib!" but there came to be a certain very pathetic inflection in the way she said it.
A large room was appropriated to her, and a local
nurse was engaged to be her attendant and companion. Thus the general arrangements of the
house were hardly altered by her addition to the
family. By a tacit understanding there had been no
meeting between Lina and the old man. Neither
had suggested it, and without that Sibbald knew
that it was far better it should not occur. He from
his physical infirmities had always been located
downstairs; she was up; so that not even by in-
direct suggestion need they be in each other's mind.

Now that he could see her closely, and at leisure,
and in a calmer frame of mind, Sibbald was more
than ever deeply moved by the tragical change in
her. Something in her behaviour (more marked at
one time than another) gave the idea of her having
undergone some critical shock : of terror, of pain, or
other high emotion that would leave an indelible im-

pression on her nerves. She showed no inclination to reveal the slightest glimpse of her existence through those missing months; and not only was her husband far from seeking such, but it was his daily prayer that she might never be impelled to make it. Sometimes when he came into her room, although the circumstances of the case never permitted him to do it suddenly, she would visibly start as he approached her, as if in fear, but instantly recognising him, she would smile, and perhaps even lay a wasted hand on his sleeve.

"I never expected all this, Sib. I don't deserve it," she said one evening, which was her strongest expression hitherto.

After she had been there a fortnight, one evening when her husband went in to her she appeared to be much brighter than usual. She asked him if he would take her for a drive. That he readily promised if she would get well enough to take it.

"And on the river?" she said with what seemed almost her old giggle.

"In a boat do you mean?" suggested Sibbald.

"Why, of course, you silly boy, how else could we go? . . . Oh, I love the river. These hot days to go lazily along, and hear the oars dipping, and let your fingers touch the water over the side, wouldn't it be divine?"

"But unfortunately our river isn't deep enough up here," said he, feeling uneasiness at her way of talking. Then looking at him, she laughed outright. But in the midst of it she checked herself, glanced at him in surprise, and appeared to be gathering the thread of some reflection. Then an expression of painful gloom settled upon her features, and she became silent.

This was the first direct indication of any uncertainty of mind in her, and it agitated Sibbald extremely. He wished to put an end to the interview, in the hope that she might rest, and he made a movement with that intention. She at once seized his hand.

"*You* are not going?" she cried with a paroxysm of terror in her features. "Don't you leave me. Everybody leaves me like that."

He said something about its being time for her to
be sleeping, and tried to turn it into a joke ; but her
eyes remained on him.

" That's not it. I know it isn't that. You want
to slip away, and how shall I find my way in this
place ? "

" Then I will stay if you wish it."

" Why, it's you, Sib ! No man was ever so good
as you."

He sat with her for some time longer, in silence
for the most part, and was only allowed at last to go
with great reluctance.   .

.   That night agitated him greatly. The figure of
his wife as she had talked to him then would not be
removed from his brain, and after he had gone early
to his bedroom he could not attempt to rest. He
had begun to undress, but after walking about un-
decidedly, and becoming aware of the cold, he
changed his mind, and pulling on his coat, went
downstairs. He piled on coal, and with the bellows
revived the fire, settling himself in a chair before it
as soon as there was a roaring glow. He sat there

a long time, lost in painful reverie, with only the silent house and the yet more silent world of frozen desolation for leagues around him.

He was quite oblivious of time in sitting there; perhaps he at length dozed. Suddenly, whether from doze or reverie, he started to his feet. It seemed to him that an agonising shriek had rent the silence of the house, and if his sensation were anything to go by, the silence of the world. He held his breath and listened, with his heart thumping in his breast, but there was no immediate repetition. That it could have been wholly imaginary he could not suppose. He passed from the room, and ran rapidly upstairs. Just as he reached Lina's door, it was opened, and the nurse in her nightgown, with a candle in her hand, came out. She was almost frightened out of her wits by the unexpected apparition.

" You must away for the doctor, Mr. Crozier," she said, when she collected herself. " Ay, ay, she's bad."

Without waiting for anything further, Sibbald sped downstairs. Scarcely had he reached the bottom before there was another cry, this time his own name, uttered in heart-rending appeal. He was up again in an instant, and within the door. The nurse met him as though she had expected that result; but she was angry, and ordered him from the room in a furious whisper, and bade him take the road.

Below, the ghastly figure of the old man, also in night attire, with a candle in his hand, intercepted him.

" Is there murder gan'ing on i' the hoose ? " cried he. Sibbald explained that his wife was ill, and that he was about to take horse, so the other withdrew, muttering something about being " fair deeved," and the " like o' that," to which his son did not stay to listen.

Swiftly the messenger, with a lantern in his hand, rode through the night. The ray from his light cleaved the solid darkness, and seemed to leave a lurid stream behind. The clang of the sparkling hoofs resounded round the hills, and was answered by distant dogs, which the rider did not hear. Never had he so ridden to Otterburn, by night or day.

Having aroused the doctor, Sibbald returned with scarcely less impetuosity. In his excited state, the blind movement seemed the only outlet to his feelings. There was fascination in the thought of riding thus madly on over the dark and ice-bound hills without end or object, mere abandonment to the winter wind. But he restrained himself, and drew rein in the yard of his merely temporal abode. When he entered the house, he found the nurse downstairs.

"She'll do," said she hastily, "but the bairn's dead." And Sibbald reflected alone, until he heard the movements of a horse outside.

For a day or two the doctor spoke hopefully of Lina's case, but Sibbald felt that he spoke more hopefully than he thought. The Scholar was himself a novice in such cases, but in the brief interviews he had been permitted with the patient, at her own urgent request, it appeared to him that her life was out. He thought she looked more beautiful than he had ever seen her, but of an unearthly, spiritual beauty. There was a placidity, too, evidently a clear coherence of thought, in her which had before been wanting. She herself told Sibbald she should not live, upon their first meeting after the crisis, and with a calm, almost glad, resignation, which contrasted forcibly with the former Adelina. There was also an odd simplicity about her, which had singular results. For instance, upon this first occasion also, she said :

"I ought never to have left you, Sibbald. I don't think there is any man like you."

She looked at him reflectively as she spoke. The sense of shame, wrong, or injury, if existing in her at all, had evidently lost all its poignancy. As her physical weakness increased, and even the doctor at the end of the week admitted that it was so, the simplicity, or obliviousness, of mind became more pronounced in her. She was occasionally playful with her husband, and a little bit coquettish. He was not allowed to read to her, with the exception of the New Testament. That pleased her, and a positive radiance of happiness would overspread her features after listening to the infinite promises.

"Say your prayers with me to-night, Sib," she said once after so listening, "for I'm sure the prayers of such a good man as you are will help me.   For I am very wicked, you know.   I am very happy now, but I am sure I'm really very wicked."

Then after he had complied, in a broken voice unaccustomed to such occasions, she took his hand whilst he was still kneeling, and stroked it, then kissed it, and as he looked up she laughed mischievously.

"You pet boy! Love me once more. Take me really in your arms. You haven't done that since I came back."

He complied immediately, a spasm of intense agony clutching at his heart, as he felt the bones of the poor wasted body.

"I have never been in love with you before," she said into his ear.

Such interviews were unspeakably distressing to Sibbald, and would leave him in a fever for the whole night. It seemed to him that only now, when she was on the point of going out, had Lina come to be a woman at all, and it induced in him a constant vein of profound musing, which was painful enough, but the reverse of melancholy.   As though to accompany

this vein in him, the heavens had cleared, and now,
early in January, there was a burst of exquisite
winter weather. Much of the snow had melted, but
it was now again clear intense frost, with a brilliant
sun. There was but little farm work, and he frequently gave up a whole morning to his reflections
out of doors. Despite the warm sun, as he walked
out his moustache became stiff with the frozen breath
in a few minutes. A gentle west wind breathed
round him, and his eyes would wander over the bright
sky, noting the long-drawn strips of cloud, the
delicate ribs and spray that rose above the grey
horizon mist. The loftier hills were still smooth and
spotless ; the smaller ones less white, showing brown
bracken and grass through the snow, and large dark
green knots of gorse. Where there was a stretch of
heather that was knee-deep, it was the white that
became scarcely visible ; darkest, deepest purple pre-
vailing over it. Fir plantations were black as coal.
Sibbald had noted all such a thousand times
throughout his life, but never in such mood as now.
Those cloudlets took "a sober colouring" from all

these late experiences, a colouring fraught with solemn, profoundly soothing, emotions.

One of these days, as he was returning from the fold in the afternoon, reflective as usual, he stopped by the yard to talk with his principal hind, whom he encountered there. Their voices were loud in the intense stillness, and a cow was lowing in the byre, but the silence of incipient twilight was upon all else. Sibbald heard a door open, but he was looking the other way, and paid no heed to it.

"They want you, sir," remarked the man, pointing to the female figure, that appeared beckoning vehemently, and Crozier went.

Adelina had summoned him, and the nurse deemed it a case of urgency.

The invalid seemed rather excited as Sibbald entered, but not quite collected in her mind.

"This isn't him," she cried. "Go back to my husband! How can I go back to him, you cruel wretch?"

A flood of painful delirium followed, from which Sibbald wished to escape, but was restrained by the nurse's entreaty.

"She was quite right just now," she said, "and wanted to see you badly. Stay a bit; she'll be right." So he withdrew aside.

The woman's expectations were fulfilled. Lina grew calmer, talked more rationally.

"It was my real husband Sibbald I wanted," said she presently. "Won't he come to me?"

"Yes, darling, I am here," he said, again stepping forward, and a flush of pleasure overspread Lina's face at the sight of him.

"Oh, Sib, I have never told you all about it," began she, much to his consternation. "I can't go away without telling you. Do come and sit by me."

"I will; but you mustn't excite yourself. You know that I understand all about it."

"But I feel that I must tell you. I have wanted to for ever such a long time." She made him come so that she could hold his hand. "I am quite safe when I hold your hand," she added, with a faint smile.

Despite the recent vagary, Crozier felt that she was more herself now than she had been at any time since her arrival. There was obviously more con-

VOL. III.   L

sciousness of a real weight upon her mind. Yet she now looked at him fearlessly again.

" I want to—"

He felt his hand convulsively clutched, and saw the corresponding change in her face. He instantly leaped up and bent over her, sheltering her in his arms, as a few days before she had begged him to.

Very soon Adelina was in repose, and had no confession to make, whilst Sibbald, not weeping, went out into the cold air. There was no wind, and the sun had just gone behind the Border hills, but still irradiated some small light bits of cloud to a golden hue, and one rosy spray above them. A few light straight lines of grey gathered around the horizons, whilst a low grey mist was settling in the valleys, showing the hill summits above. Through the subdued light in which all the landscape was enveloped, the top of Carter Fell was intensely clear.

Sibbald leaned on the gate to watch it, and saw those cloudlets turn into brilliant crimson. He was still there when they were dead.

CHAPTER VII.

THE FATES.

THE parting with Adelina affected Crozier more than might have been supposed. Never in any but a legal sense married to her, and so soon altogether separated in so effectual a way, the case seemed but to demand a very moderate degree of mourning. In the strict sense of the term, no doubt a very scant portion of mourning was allotted to it, but wreaths and hat-bands did not dispose of the matter in the mind of this impressionable youth. Whilst the friction of a daily incompatible existence with Adelina had been constantly upon him, she only lived to emphasise by contrast a certain ideal of which she herself could not claim one single ray. Oddly enough, now that she had come and died with him, the position of things was almost exactly reversed. The ideal upon which he had then sustained his being was dim, scarcely existent; the despised one reigned supreme.

But the change was not what on the surface it seemed to be. If that pathetic figure of the shattered Lina did now persistently haunt him, instead of what had haunted him before, it was not that she had resumed her position as woman in his heart. It was only that by her suffering she had been able to displace woman altogether there. The purely emotional shock had extinguished love in him for a time. The old ideal in all its glory was still essentially a woman; the new, simply an enthusiastic conception of the soul.

From the divinity of Love he had gone on to the divinity of Pity, and circumstances could not but connect the latter with the dying beauty of the departed.

From the purely selfish passion he had passed to a broader one, and it became a vital force in his development as a creature of this world. After the first consuming agitation was over, he found himself looking around with a vastly widened sympathy upon the world at large. In the course of life to which he was pledged, his immediate world was a narrow one, but in human essentials it was as typical as any. Love, hatred, gladness, misery, knowledge and ignorance, these occur wheresoever two or three are gathered together, and so it was in the valley of the Rede. In his first months at Whaup-riggs his reputation for mysterious pride and exclusiveness seemed to have flown over from the Braid water. From that January, however, dated a change. He began to be spoken of in rather a respectful way as a singularly well-meaning fellow.

His education had been limited, having gone only so far as the elementary teacher of a remote school-house in Braiddale could take it ; but it had fallen on to intelligent ground, and had prepared the way, to be wholly superseded by a generous, if immethodical, love of books. Thus it was that his imagination and emotions had been developed to a so much larger extent than his intellect, and that consequently it was in no new and startling "scheme" that his new fervour was to be manifested. The oldest and simplest sufficed him.

In the course of the next three years there Sibbald came to be associated with all the social work of his valley. Although he identified himself with Horsley Church he was soon well known as a wholly un-sectarian enthusiast, to whom the common needs of mankind formed the first recommendation. One of his most intimate friends was an elder of the Presby-terian Church. So far as old Crozier knew anything of this activity, it aroused in him a surly resentment. With the progress of time the old man's theory and practice had become utterly inconsistent. Although, if anybody had been inconsiderate enough to charge him with it, he would still have held to his confession that he was a cuckoo in his nest, he none the less daily spoke and acted as if the fullest Crozier pre-rogative was still his own. It was certainly in this capacity that he scorned his son's later proceedings ; for to the genuine Crozier nothing could be more con-temptible than systematic philanthropy. You might as well be a minister at once, and a Crozier in the black garb,—but happily, even this last degenerate member was spared such an excruciating display as that.

In spite of this subject of contention (perfectly well known to Sibbald, although never in the most distant manner alluded to), he managed to find a good deal to have in common with his father. It was soon plain that his pastoral enterprise was to succeed, and for the promotion of its best qualities nobody was better equipped than " aa'd Crozier." In these respects his judgment seemed wholly unimpaired. He could discuss the merits of the relative breeds, even of the individual famous flocks, as vigorously as at any time in his life. Sibbald consequently received the most valuable advice in the selection of his purchases, and the deference to him naturally pleased and tended to soothe the old man. Physically, however, the latter did not greatly improve. He could hobble about the farm on two sticks, but it seemed as though beyond that he was never again to be permitted to go.

In various ways, therefore, the name of the new

tenant of Whaupriggs was soon noised abroad in a very complimentary manner, reaching amongst other places his native valley of the Braid. In various households there he was discussed, and amongst the rest in that of Angryhaugh. Those detached bits of intercourse which the shepherd, Curle, had had with Crozier had considerably modified his opinion of him, and these later reports fully confirmed the alteration.

"That Scholar's nae gowk after a'," he would remark to his wife when he was in a mood for breaking his habitual taciturnity. "I doubt he'll come ower to the right kirk at the hinder end."

"Varry likely," would the wife reply. "He seems quite a canny fellow. It's a tarr'ble shame that he should ha' lost Bygate."

"Tarr'ble strange affair that," assented the man. "I could never get to the bottom on't."

"Ou, it was just along of his marrying the lassie. Isabel told me, ye ken. Ye'll mind I tellt ye a' about it."

"Ay, ay, what they said," remarked the shepherd

imperturbably. "But they dinna aye get at the truth, ye ken. Aa'd Crozier was ower fond o' the place to dea it for the like o' that. He had lost a deal o' cash I'm thinking, although I canna mak' it oot."

"They said that man Felton had robbed him of twae thousand pounds," interposed Jenniper, who sat silent as a rule whilst this subject was discussed.

"Ay, ay, my lassie, but Crozier would no hae to sell Bygate for the loss o' twae thousand pounds. He had mair like ten thousand in the investments. That ne'er-do-weel fallow Hislop would aye have it that Felton had robbit him of a good deal mair, and that he was juist the lassie's father, wha they made believe was dead."

"Well, David, ye hae never told me that before," exclaimed the mother in a reproachful tone. "Did you ken o' that, Jenniper?"

"Ou, ay, I heard 'em talk about it."

"Ay, but I'd never believe that lad Hislop. He was a most awfu' liar, and if he couldna get ony ill of a body he'd *mak'* it. I dinna believe half o' what he said about young Crozier an' a'. It was a good day for ye, Jenniper, when ye were aff wi' him."

"Aff, indeed!" cried Jenniper indignantly. "I was never on, mother. They were all his lies that said sae."

"Ay, ay, nae doubt," gravely assented the man. "He is juist yane o' the lost sheep. They tell me that he was put away frae that Yorkshire place for poaching himsel'. I aye suspeckit him here. And William Henderson told me the day that he was through to Crawston but twa-three days sin' for a' the world like a common tramp."

And so the conversation would travel on to the infinite satisfaction of the housewife, to whom such snatches were a godsend, and but a flash in the darkness of elemental silence.

Jenniper rose from such a conversation with a sense of depression. Any mention of Sibbald Crozier's name, any glimpse of it in the local paper, made her heart beat faster even still, although it was three years since she set eyes on him, and longer since she had vehemently resolved to banish him from her mind. Whether she would or no, the Scholar (practically since she met him at the Howff with the lantern) had crept into her mind as an ideal of the race, and neither marriage, nor time, nor her own determination, had been able to shake his position there. She was not a girl to shed daily tears of sensibility over her hopeless dream, but, no doubt, for her rescue from the predicament it would have been very much better if she had been. In that case perhaps some other comforter might have been found. As it was, she remained a profound mystery to all about her, with the exception that is of Maggie Laidler. Nobody could fathom her secret, and yet it was so obvious that *the* change had now for a long time come over her. She was watched; she was courted; but with equal fruitlessness. Latterly she had had to be left alone, which was very much to her own satisfaction.

With the muscular Maggie she still retained her intimacy, and she had an opportunity in the afternoon which followed the above scrap of dinner talk of going to her friend's cottage. Directly she stepped inside, and received the glance of the middle-aged woman, she saw that there was something in the latter's features. The expression was altogether different from the customary hard, fixed frown. It almost suggested gladness, in a comparative degree.

"What did ye promise?" demanded Maggie with affected sternness none the less. "Ye hae been thinking on him."

"I had come to tell you that I canna keep my promise, that I winna keep it. I'll fling it ower the Foulburn Knowe. I'll think o' the lad just when I like, and as often as I like. There's naething else in the world worth thinking about."

"It's an uncanny thing this love, as ye ca' it," mused Maggie contemptuously. "But—but I'll tell ye yae thing, hinny. Ye hae got a real good lad in your fancy."

"Ha, ha!" laughed Jenniper derisively, and with prolonged triumph. "Sae even you come out o' your scorner's chair! We'll hae miracles, Maggie, by and by." And again the girl abandoned herself to a triumphant peal.

" Ay, a real good lad," interposed Maggie when she could. " But he's no a Crozier, ye ken."

" I dinna care what he is. He's a braw, bonnie laddie, and what do I care for his name ? Ca' him Jock if ye hae a mind to."

" And ye may ha'd him in your mind, Jennie ; and get a ha'd of him in your arms, too, lass, if ye hae the skeel to."

Jenniper frowned, and looked to the doorway· offended.

" And I'll help ye, lass."

" What do you mean ? " demanded the other, without the smallest relaxation of feature.

" Ay, he is a good, bonnie laddie, and I never thought to say sae much for ony Crozier that could come ower the doorstane o' Bygate. I hae seen him wi' these een the day, lass."

" Nae wonder you look sae heartsome, Maggie," said Jenniper, turning quickly round. " Where ha' you been ? Tell me a' about it. Come, quick ! "

" Ay, we canna be quick enough now I'll warrant.

Well, I was just ower the hill to my sister Dodds at Skirlnakit."

"But he wasna there? . . . Go on, Maggie. I canna stay a' night wi' you."

"No, he wasna there; but he cam' there when I was ben. Sicna yald fellow he's grown to! I hardly kent him, although he was never just that scrimp, daur say. Well, and it's just this, Jenniper, he's to be there on Saturday forenoon; I heard him say sae, and—and ye'll hae to be along that gate just by accident, ye ken."

"What does he gan there for?" asked the girl, as if by no means wholly satisfied with the suggestion.

"Well, ye ken, Bella's gan to flit, since George is dead, and they hae some disagreement wi' the maister about George's flock, and it's just ower this that the lad's come to see that she's no wranged. Pringle is the hardest and maist tyrannical body i' the whole world, and they a' ken it. But he'll no wheezle yon lad."

"But I'll no gan," suddenly interposed Jenniper, with vehemence. "I'll no gan. I canna gan. He'd ken it. What have I to do there? He kens that I never gan."

" Ha'd a wee, lass! I just told Bella that ye were coming up yae day soon, aiblins next week. What for canna ye gan the last day o' this? Ay, ay, he heard it. I took good care o' that. . . . Do ye think I'm a fool? I just threw it in at the hinder end, quite ordinary. ' Is that Jenniper Curle?' said he, turning to me quick, for I didna say the Curle. ' Ay, ay, sir,' I said, ' ye'll mind her, daur say?' ' I should think I do,' said he, wi' a bonnie smile; . and though I'm an aa'd woman noo, Jen, I ken a bonnie smile yet brawly."

"You're no aa'd, Maggie, you're no aa'd," cried Jenniper, clutching her companion round the neck. " You're just the best and bonniest woman that ever was in a' the Braiddale."

" Well, ha'd aff, hinny — I canna speak. The smile's no a'. I'll tak' my dying aith, but there was a wee blush till it. . . . Ha'd away wi' you! Dinna I ken that his cheek's bonnie enough ony way, but it went all ower his face. . . . Do you think I'd lee to ye in sicna maitter?" said the woman, in real sternness, to which the other bowed, and was silent. "It was as I tell ye, and as soon as I saw it, I said to mysel', 'Yon lass is in the right o't yet.' And sae ye are, Jenniper lass, and I hae been just a fool for yance. But a Crozier? Nay, I canna mak' it oot."

"But I canna gan; I winna gan," declared Jenniper again, and kept declaring it at intervals as long as she remained.

The whole of the afternoon was sacrificed, and it was tea-time before the girl flitted back across the bent in the sinking March sun, all her frame quivering with excitement at the result of the interview. But go she should not. The trick was open, shameless. And yet how—how was she ever to see him again? . . . And *now* she might. He was free. Hadn't she hugged the words for years now? In no coarse triumph over the dead, but—oh, with an infinitude of tremulous emotion. Even when he was *not* free, hadn't he called her "an angel of light?"— words never forgotten—never to be forgotten. But he was a different man now. She knew it—was sure of it. A far, far better man ; a man to die for—or to live.

Accordingly, the following Saturday morning, a frosty March morning, whilst all the grass blades glittered with their silvery rime, Jenniper was away up the hill. A good four-mile, bleak, and desolate walk was before her, but had it been under the same conditions as when last she drove it with him behind her, it would have been to Jenniper brilliant enough. As it was to-day, every diamond and amethyst that sparkled to the sun over those barren leagues had its reflection in her heart ; every note that showered from the mad glee of the venturous larks, its fellow in every string of her girlish frame. At the top she struck a track over a piece of dark heathery moor, a rough, stony cart-road, in parts thickly sanded with that most priceless of all sand, formed by the crumbling of the very stone between the fingers of the elements, and every single grain of which is in the morning sun a twinkling brilliant.

So glad was she, that Jenniper would sit occasionally on a fragment of stone, and take up a handful of

the sand, letting it run glittering to the ground again
or she would pull out a bit of moss, or of the grey
feathery lichen which carpeted the earth in the shade
of the long heather, and throw it away again. She
herself alone there with the sun, the curlews, and the
grouse; and " I should think I do " the jubilant
burden of every song.

Jenniper reached the house of Mrs. Dodds at last,
a remote and solitary house, where solitude is
normal. She had acquaintance with the woman as a
member of the congregation, and, from her intimacy
with the sister Maggie, felt familiarly towards her.
Nevertheless, she approached her to-day with nervous terror. She had with the utmost difficulty,
with constant turns and irresolution, come to the
house at all when once it was in sight. But the
basket and the message from Maggie had ultimately
triumphed.

It had been a grave question with Jenniper how
long she was to stay, to which, upon her arrival, she
had obtained no answer. It was evident, therefore,
that things must take their course, and she must be

guided wholly by circumstances. When, however, she had been seated for upwards of an hour with Mrs. Dodds, feasting upon buttered girdle cakes and milk, and sustaining, as best she might, a reasonable share in the conversation, the question refused to be put aside any longer. Two hours proved amply sufficient to exhaust the wrongs to which Mrs. Dodds was being subjected by an extortionate, if not deliberately unjust, master, as well as to inspect the few ducks and poultry which she boasted. Pressure was not wanted for her just to make herself comfortable and stay until the afternoon, but, however treacherous the inclination, this Jenniper did firmly resist. When the third hour was nearly exhausted, and what might be strictly called the forenoon completely so, she set off on her homeward journey.

It was evident that, despite Maggie's sagacious artifice, she had not enlightened her sister as to the nature of it, for otherwise it is difficult to believe that Jenniper would have been allowed to depart in the face of so weighty a disappointment. Had Mrs. Dodds at all suspected the high nature of the encounter, there was nothing simpler than to see that Mr. Crozier had been unavoidably detained, and that he would come over later, until which time her visitor could be completely at her ease. Not suspecting it, after displaying ordinary persuasion, she set her visitor on her way.

Having formed the resolution, and, in the dull agony of disappointment, Jenniper was only too eager to escape. Should he arrive now at the last moment, when all her spirit had evaporated, she would be taken at a disadvantage, and the meeting would be anything but what she had looked for. Therefore, when once away, she walked with impetuous haste over that part of the moor which the house commanded, and did not once look back. The road beyond, by which Sibbald would arrive, was only visible for a very short distance.

It was not long before a horseman appeared upon it, and as he approached the house he saw, some half mile ahead, a figure moving over the moor, but it was not recognisable, and he thought no more of it as he turned up to the house. He was engaged there

about an hour, also having some refreshment, and as
the afternoon continued fine, he expressed his intention of riding on to the next ridge, just to have a
peep into Braiddale before turning home.

"Oh, I had Jenniper Curle frae Angryhaugh here
just before you came," said Mrs. Dodds. "You
might hae held her company part o' the lanesome
road, but she couldna' stay."

"What, she was here to-day?"

"Had but just gane when you got here."

"Then I saw her on the road in the distance," replied Sibbald immediately. "I am so sorry I missed
her. I should very much have liked to have seen
her again."

"I would ha' kept her if I had kent that," said the
woman as Crozier was riding away. He muttered
some answer, and they parted.

It was a singular disappointment to Sibbald, for it
chanced that he had thought a good deal of Jenniper
since Maggie Laidler's casual mention of her in his
hearing. He had even hoped that he might thus
accidentally meet her at Mrs. Dodds' house, since she

was evidently in the habit of visiting there. He therefore rode on now in a spirit of vexation. In all probability he should not be over here again, for the matter which brought him must soon be settled, and it was just the element of accident which would have made the meeting so particularly agreeable.

On account of this, Crozier paid less heed to his surroundings than was his custom. He would have cantered or galloped had there been the slightest probability of his overtaking Jenniper, but it was upwards of an hour ago. She would be descending into Braiddale by this time. So he allowed his horse to walk leisurely onwards whilst he indulged his thoughts.

The silence here seemed to him even to surpass that of Redesdale, and the step of his horse on the sandy track scarcely broke it. Such few sounds as emphasised the stillness he heard, as Jenniper had done just before him, but when he came to a certain part of the road, his ear caught something different. Impossible as it appeared to him, he was yet convinced that it was human voices. Before completely deciding it in his mind, all doubt was immediately removed by a most unmistakable human shriek. His horse started at the sound as much as he did, and Sibbald leaped to the ground. To the left the ground here descended rather abruptly to a defile down which ran a tributary of the Braid. In the slope was another crease, which at a short distance was filled with birch and alder trees. It was from this part that Sibbald thought the sound had come. Leaving his horse where it was, he darted down the slope at a perilous pace. A score of strides brought him to where the trees began. He had not to enter far before coming to the object of his search, and his whole soul quivered within him. A branch of a tree which the storms had broken was against his foot, and in an instant he had grasped it. Like a tiger, he sprang forward in pursuit of a figure which had turned in terrified flight. The twigs snapped beneath their feet, and one blow from Crozier's weapon had felled the creature that he hunted. This seemed, however, only to inflame the anger that was in him, and a pitiless shower of strokes continued to descend upon the prostrate figure, from which came howls and shrieks which rent the silence of the hills for miles. Probably weary with his frenzied exertion, Sibbald paused, and with his foot thrust the object of his fury into the stony channel of the burn. With nostrils dilated, lips apart, whence came his heavy pants, and all his features aflame, Crozier eyed his victim as though meditating another spring. In reality he only looked to see that he was alive. Of this he was soon satisfied, for the man crawled out of the water on the opposite side, and taking, as he thought, un-perceived, a large stone in his hand, he flung it full at his antagonist, whom it fortunately only hit in the middle of the chest. For an instant it made Crozier reel, but steadying himself, he likewise grasped a missile, but the other was descending the slope.

"I give you three hours," shouted Sibbald after him. "In that time the police will be on your track."

Then he stood for an instant as though appreciating his victory.

When he turned to reascend, Crozier saw Jenniper

standing where he had passed her, only she had raised her hand to lay it on a branch of alder. She was looking down intently towards him. An expression of some high emotion, which might have been terror or extreme astonishment, was on her face, but it changed as he ascended. With every step he took the colour in those features deepened, but when he was beside her it had almost gone. Very beautiful Jenniper looked just then as she glanced fully but timidly into his face. He showed signs of his recent paroxysm of rage, but a smile rode over them as he gazed, simply gazed, calmly into Jenniper's eyes as though to construe them. It was but for a second, but a second involving endless time, an endless issue.

"Jenniper," he said, taking one more step.

"Yes, Sibbald," said she, and his arms closed around her.

For the rest of her journey Jenniper had company, and Hislop did not again appear.

CHAPTER VIII.

BRETT, DECEASED.

For the next fortnight Crozier and Jenniper heard nothing whatever about each other. They had been so supremely startled into that revelation, that when they came afterwards to contemplate it, they were overwhelmed with a sense of astonishment and shame. A glow of tremulous joy, to be sure, burned underneath it ; but it seemed impossible to each that *so* this supreme, this unattainable, climax had been reached. It must have been owing to some individual unworthiness that so abrupt a method had been found. Long and solemn preparation seemed in the fitness of things to lead up to such a summit, whereas they had clutched it at one swoop of their sacrilegious wings. To nobody as yet had they revealed it, in set terms not even to themselves. For the remainder of their journey to Angryhaugh, they had simply talked in ardent, intimate manner, as though all was understood without any express terms. What *had* they to express after that one silent meeting of the lips?

Nevertheless, each of them looked with tremulous dismay to the next meeting, and so it was that it did not come about. Sibbald devoted himself with feverish energy to his agricultural and other pursuits, Jenniper to her simpler household duties. Not even to Maggie Laidler did the latter repair, very much to the astonishment of Maggie. But in such a matter she considered that no news was good news, so she dwelt content.

Thus the remainder of March escaped them.

Upon the first Sunday in April, Maggie observed that David Curle and his wife went down the hill together, that Jenniper, therefore, was left presumably alone. Upon such an irresistible invitation, curiosity became too strong, and she, all ready as she was, resolved to omit her own walk to Crawston this Sabbath, and go to see what the mystery might portend. So, as soon as the others were out of sight, to Angryhaugh she turned her steps.

Jenniper saw the figure pass the window, and a thrill of excitement shot through her frame. Was she or was she not to confess it? What had she to confess? He had not even said, " I love you," much less, " Will you be my wife? " Maggie walked in.

" Well, ye are a fine lass, ye are ! " was her first remark. " Daur say I thought ye had perished in the cleugh."

The woman cast a shrewd and penetrating glance upon Jenniper, which the other tried to evade.

" I ken a' aboot it, lass. When is it to be ? The like o' ye 'ull no need mony days to mak' ready. Come, find your tongue ! " And Maggie sat down.

Jenniper burst into a laugh.

" Then ye're just gaun ower quick. A' we hae come to is just naething at a'."

" That's tarr'ble likely," was the laconic rejoinder. " Then let's ken the naething at a'. Did ye see the lad ? "

Jenniper's face burnt. The start which Crozier

had given him was apparently sufficient for Hislop's purpose, for nothing whatever had been heard of him since. The circumstances of the encounter, therefore, were a profound secret from all except those who had had a part in them, and so, no doubt, would remain always.

"Ay, daur say I saw him," replied the girl carelessly.

"Come, my lass," said Maggie, in an altered tone, a tone of genuine kindness. "Hae ye made a start?"

"I dinna ken what we hae done."

"Then it'll do," said the other complacently. "Ye'll soon ken mair."

Jenniper's face afforded in itself sufficient information, so Maggie pestered her no more. She began to talk of general things.

Still, day after day went by, and Jenniper did not "ken mair." At last a real anxiety was beginning to disturb her. Had he, in fact, already repented of his impulsive movement? Of his intense excitement there was no doubt. Had his simple, generous emotion carried him too far, and he now knew not

how to disown it? The thought rose up before her
like a terrifying cloud.   Such terrific storms and
thunder lurked within it that she dared not give it a
direct look.   Her instinct rather was to rush to any
shelter, and simply hide her head.   And yet—and
yet, the cloud might altogether pass, and she escape
it.   She was thrown into an agony of doubt.

The disquiet corresponded to no uncertainty in
Crozier, except the tender uncertainty of how to act.
The discovery had come upon his life with such a
glory, that he was simply ignorant of how the days
went by.   His own fervour sustained him.   No doubt
the agitating circumstances of their first meeting had
re-impressed Jenniper's image upon him with overwhelming force.   He had begun again to think of
her in a vague, aspiring way ; but so it might have
continued for an indefinite time had not that episode
occurred to rouse him.   In an instant the personal
element was forced upon him ; the actual, the
existing woman was in his mind, and as it had
been presented, it immediately found dormant
forces with which to combine.   Vivid, glowing life

in its intensest attributes was again in his veins.
He could not, nay, he would not, quell them. An
ideal, a transcendental, glory sustained him; but not
a mystical. He could place the ghostly beauty of an
Adelina beside this loving, throbbing one, and see
the issues without a tremor.

In the midst of this enthusiasm, and whilst coming
rapidly to a conclusion how to act, one morning a
letter was delivered to him, which struck strangely
upon the high tension of his frame. He thought he
knew the handwriting, but was willing to admit a
doubt. It was on this account that he handled and
re-handled the missive in a subdued, an abstracted,
way, as he strode off to a secret part to peruse it. It
clashed, nevertheless, with both his ideals in an unpleasant way, introducing what was antagonistic to
either. He examined the envelope; in quality it
was good. That fact he noted. The postmark, too,
—Newcastle-on-Tyne. The very name thus presented did not suggest the brightest reminiscences,
although actively even they could not in any sense
subdue him. But all his emotions of late had been

enthusiastically generous, in the widest sense of the term. Those here suggested were ignoble, if he himself would not have used a stronger word. But he tore the paper. To Crozier's astonishment (for when he had opened it he glanced first at the signature), the letter was written upon the printed stationery of one of the principal Newcastle hotels, and it ran thus :—

" DEAR SIBBALD,—I had hardly expected this. It is hard to have come through a weary voyage, imposed upon me as the only chance of life, and when I am home at last, to be told that I must die. Such is my condition, and although I am far from repining at the dispensations of a Providence which has blessed me far far beyond my deserts, I had so earnestly hoped that, at least, a few months would have been vouchsafed me here. The doctors assure me that it is not to be, and, indeed, I feel very clearly that they speak the truth. Therefore, as a dying man upon whom many former sins lie as an intolerable burden, may I ask you to forgive me all that is past, and so far show me mercy as to come and give me a parting word. I have nobody else that I can ask, or that I would ask. If you come, come alone. I dare not at first see *her*. Nay, do not let her know that I am here until I have seen you. I may live a week ; it is not thought possible for two. God always bless you.

" Affectionately yours,

" CHARLES FELTON."

Sibbald's eyes remained upon the paper after he had read it in absent thought. The words affected him, for despite the signature he could not but feel that there was a plaintive ring of human sincerity in them. How much of his past life did the man's name awaken ! Brief in duration, and to his sense infinite ages ago, yet was it at the root of his conscious existence still.

But the more ignoble surprise and speculation could not be excluded long. Was it possible that he had flourished in so short a time? Clearly no travelling fiddler would take up his quarters at the Atlas

Hotel. But Felton respectable and with means! Sympathy had to succumb to his sense of humour, and Crozier laughed aloud. At any rate, he was delivered from his very worst impressions.

He decided to respond to the summons forthwith, so easily making some excuse for his absence, he set off that morning to Newcastle. He had never set foot there since his first departure with his father to Redesdale, so his arrival was a strange experience. Old ghosts thronged busily about him, but despite their frowns, he found that all their terrors had departed. He could stare them in the face, and they fled. From a more broadly human point of view, too, his attitude had altered, and he looked with great interest around, but a thrill of satisfaction passed through him as he thought of his pastures at home. To this he felt still a stranger with whatever curiosity he might look.

The imposing hotel was, indeed, such as he had thought it. He inquired for the invalid, and was received with deference, somebody being told off to conduct him to the apartment. As he ascended the

staircase Sibbald regarded the luxury about him
with wonder, and to associate Felton with it passed
his ability. Thoughts of their old conversations
came back to him, of so-called philosophies on his
part, "of new beginnings; disappointments new."
They were like reminiscences of some other world.
He was taken into a room that looked to him like a
sumptuous drawing-room, and there he was left. A
minute or two later a pretty nurse with becoming
cap and apron appeared, and said Mr. Felton would
see him at once. So Sibbald followed into an adjoining room.

All was upon the same amazing scale: silence,
fragrance, and glitter all around. Observation of de-
tail Crozier did not attempt. On entering the bedroom his eyes naturally first fell upon the bed, but its
beautiful hangings only enshrouded a spotless un-
ruffled contour, the repose of which *he* certainly
would not have dared to break even to obtain his
own. A voice which he recognised at once greeted
him from another part of the room, and turning, he
saw a figure enfolded in a crimson dressing-gown re-

clining on the softest and easiest of couches, but as Felton he would not at once have known it.

As Sibbald advanced towards him, the invalid rose slowly from his place, despite the visitor's entreaty, and extended his hand.   When he had folded the other in it he covered it also with his left, and so held Crozier for some time in silent paternal benediction.   It was evident that some genuine emotion prevented his speech, for after one look into Sibbald's eyes he had to lower his own.

What had made so great an alteration in him was his beard, which he had allowed to grow again.   But upon this close inspection Sibbald saw it to be the right man.   His face was very thin, and through his brilliant attire his whole frame had the appearance of being much emaciated.   Anybody in such a plight would have awakened Crozier's sympathy, and this man no less than another.   He spoke warmly of what he felt, and his words only increased the other's agitation.   But, at length, they both sat down.

"I have much to say to you, my boy," began Felton when he was able.   "I don't know how I shall do it. I did not think it would be so bad as this. But, at least, you—you see I have prospered."

Sibbald assented, and looked around the room once more, commenting upon the comfort.

"There is no place for privacy and comfort like a good hotel," Felton went on, easing his position on the couch. "I have tried various places and circumstances, and have found none to approach it. . . . But I must tell you all. I—I—must— Your father? Is he—"

"Fairly well," said Crozier, not deeming it necessary to disquiet the unfortunate man by adverse particulars.

"He is! . . . Oh, the mercies are manifold! Thank God, it has fallen upon myself, but that, too, tempered more marvellously than I can tell you. You knew of the crimes under which we started?" It seemed almost a flash of anger in his eyes.

"But it was Curle—"

"I equally with him. Yes, yes, equally, for it is not for me to apportion the guilt. We have both had to pay the penalty. *He* was killed by an accidental explosion two years ago. I—I am spared —at least to see you, Sibbald."

The casual announcement of the hapless Daniel's fate impressed Sibbald as odd, if nothing further, but to it he did not allude.

"And to do more, I hope," said he as a purely sympathetic commonplace, but he saw that his companion eyed him closely. "Doctors have been cheated before this."

"Ay, ay," returned Felton with a sigh, apparently of relief; "but I am not to cheat them. I feel the doom upon me—but, Sibbald, I shall—shall do more," he suddenly exclaimed with access of energy, and giving way even to a feeble smile. "More, perhaps, than even you think. Do you know I am a rich man? But of that presently. The other is the vital part. Not only rich. I am an altered man."

Crozier nodded, speculating more and more as to what was to come. . . . Rich!

"You will remember our old talks? . . . But for

my crimes I should never have been delivered from
them. The *new life* I was ever demanding, thinking
(you recollect) that it lay in deliverance from old
circumstances. It is to the madness, the criminality,
of *that* that I am awake. From that arose all the
crimes, all the frustration, of a useless life. The
change I wanted incessantly was the outward, deeming as the veriest truism that the inward must follow.
It is all a delusion, a snare of the devil. The only
change that can come is from within first; upon that
anything can follow; without it, nothing but—such
as I have been."

The man seemed to weary himself with his decla-
mation, but he would only pause to take a few deeper
breaths.

" I was even induced to rob your father under this
demoniac impression that any means would justify
the desired end,—the new, the spiritual life. *He,*
subtly enough, as I have since seen, played upon
that, urged that there could be no change so funda-
mental as a changed world, an altered hemisphere. I
was persuaded, and behold, it wrought my salvation.

When I arrived there and got settled, I found it was no change. The same anxieties, the same feverish aspirations, haunted me still. Then, in a vision of the night, believe it or not as you like, I was awakened,—I heard as from a voice omnipotent, "The change is from within!" It came upon me like a flash of light. I felt the truth of it, and from that moment, as indeed I then cried aloud, " I am a changed man ! "

Again he paused to breathe, and Sibbald regarded in silence what he could not but consider as an innocent form of mania.

"I rose from my bed a changed man. One, and one violent conviction only possessed me—the enormity of my sin. Then I saw that the world's life-long accusations were true in substance and in fact. A bankrupt, a thief, a common felon, I was ; this and no other. For a time I was utterly crushed, pulverised by the magnitude of the conviction. Rebound seemed impossible. Death and hell stared me in the face. But," he added, with a smile of ineffable calmness, " you see I was raised. The hand

in which I trusted raised me, and I am here—ready,
yes, ready to take that further journey which he
demands of me. Resolution returned. Whilst a
moment's breath remained to me for one thing only
did I live: restitution, as far as foul lucre could
effect it, of all the wrong that I had done. For that
only I lived, and for it I am content to die. Everything assisted me. God was with me in the mines,
and what else did I require? I now return to you a
rich man. If I could have stayed another year I
could have added to my riches tenfold, but it is
enough. I shall not die a bankrupt, and felony God
can forgive, as all else."

In the face of this singular confession it was impossible for Crozier not to be agitated by selfish
thoughts. Now that the man's object was revealed
to him, what did it not mean? He did not dare to
follow it to the issue, his tremulous excitement was
too great. But Felton saw in his eye something of
its effect, and it afforded him the balm of a viaticum.
Nevertheless, his own excessive emotion was only
too plain, and at length Sibbald felt obliged to refer

to it. He counselled rest, and promised to come again. Felton shook his head.

"Just a few minutes more," pleaded he, but there was a knock at the door, and the nurse entered.

Felton persisted, and she withdrew.

"What are a few hours?" said he with resignation. "Sibbald, I have left everything to you. Every penny is at your disposal, and you are a just man. You—will—"

His suffering had grown more apparent for some time now, but it was with a shock of alarm that Crozier saw him seized with a paroxysm of anguish. As the man's head fell back, Sibbald summoned the nurse.

"He has only fainted," she said, running up to him. "But you must go."

He stood by to be assured of a return to consciousness, and then, before he could be observed, he escaped from the room.

A fever was in the man's blood, and he walked the streets as in a dream. Rich—repair! What did he call rich? What repair? T-to buy Bygate for

instance ? Sibbald dared not formulate the question
in terms. He had so settled down to those long
patient years of toil, illuminated lately by the rays
from an unexpected glory, until the pounds should
have been slowly gathered, and then, perhaps, as a
middle-aged man claiming from Lord Braiddale, or
his successor, the promise which had been made to
him so magnanimously : to all this had he so naturally settled down, that it seemed like wanton cruelty
of fate to interpose now with a mad hope which most
likely could never be fulfilled. If Felton had been a
self-deluding maniac once, was it not possible, probable, that he was one still—that the whole of his
revelation was yet but a fiction of the brain, from
which nothing short of final extinction could ever
release him ? Such fears to Sibbald were irresistible.
Accustomed only to the methods in the byways of
the old world, in the face of such it seemed incredible
to him that a man could have accumulated anything
considerable in so short a space of time. Consequently, he went back to Redesdale in a most un-
quiet frame of mind. His plans for going over to

Jenniper were again dispelled, for until this new fever
was off his mind he could face no such high enterprise as that.   He had not long to wait.

The day after the next one he received another
communication, this time from the doctor who had
attended Felton, to state that the latter was dead.
That no doubt the excitement of the interview had
slightly accelerated the event, but as regards the
patient, had saved him from much pain, as he had
scarcely been conscious at all since Crozier left him.
He briefly explained the severe internal malady from
which the man had suffered, and concluded by beg-
ging Sibbald to come and see him with what speed
was convenient, as Felton had entrusted the writer
with all his papers.

To this summons Sibbald responded with equal
alacrity.   Upon him devolved all the necessary
funeral arrangements, as well as such testamentary
affairs as Felton himself had referred to.   The will
was found as he had stated, made briefly and exclusively in Sibbald's favour.   With this document,
however, was a paper in the form of a letter to

Crozier, expressing the wish of the deceased that indirectly all his former debts should be paid without divulging the fact of his having outlived his bankruptcy, and that Bygate, if at all possible, should be re-bought. It was added that his estate would be found sufficient for all this, and still leave a moderate sum to be Sibbald's own property. To show it there followed details of what that estate consisted, of which the sum total below, doubly underlined very methodically with ruled lines, was the principal item. This was £19,560 10s. 6d.

Not sharing his father's idiosyncrasies, Sibbald saw that the first thing to be done was to consult a lawyer, and none so naturally occurred to him as his father's former adviser, Mr. Maxwell, in Collingwood Street. To him he repaired, explained that Felton was simply a colonial returned home, and knowing him, as a relative of the late Hugh Collingwood Brett, deceased, to have expressed a desire that that bankrupt's debts should be discharged in full, gave directions forthwith to that end accordingly.

After consultation with that gentleman, and re-

ceiving his assurance that the securities were undoubtedly genuine, and would certainly realise the
sum which was stated, Sibbald designed a little private
piece of business on his own account. Now in very
truth he might approach Jenniper, without another
day, without another moment's delay. He decided
accordingly to return home by way of Braiddale, and
call at Angryhaugh to dispose of the matter.

All the valley of the Braid was a dell of gold as
Sibbald rode into it that afternoon of April. His
heart rose as he beheld it once again in such a
flood of glory, one which harmonised so well with
his own spirit. What schemes and aspirations accompanied him as he rode along on the Bygate side
(for a near glimpse of the place now was irresistible)!
What hopes and prayers as he glanced across at the
little house on the opposite slope! It was by no
means that all the later years and experiences of his
life fell from him; it was that they all clung the
closer about him, intensifying his joy. Without them
he now knew that he could never have attained to such
profundity of transport. From the darkest of them

had he gained something to aid in the transformation of a lonely enthusiast to a buoyant, sympathetic fellow of his kind. His poor old father even danced sympathetically in his imagination. Nothing, he knew, but breaking could have touched that gnarled old trunk, and better broken, he felt in his present mood, than flourishing in ignoble sturdiness. Even he should lie across his patrimonial acres, in which, everything notwithstanding, Sibbald knew full well that the roots still were fixed.

After satisfying this emotion, Crozier turned his horse down the slope and made for the river, to cross exactly opposite the Howff. The water was the richest rosy brown as it danced over the pebbles, and as his horse stepped into the current, a dipper flew away up the stream, uttering its clear, shrill whistle as it sped. The noise startled a heron higher up, and Sibbald, from mid-stream, watched the majestic fisher rise.

Another also was watching it, unknown to him, and him with it ; had been watching since he turned his horse downward from the ridge. Her eyes were often over to Bygate, and a strange figure could immediately arrest her gaze. She had had a strong conviction that he would approach her from that side, and could it be possible that he was at last to come? When there could no longer be any doubt, Jenniper turned hurriedly into her dwelling, where her mother alone was at work.

"Mother, Mr. Sibbald's coming up the brae," she cried.

"Well, lass," said her mother, looking up in astonishment at the tone, "is there sae muckle in that?"

"Ay, he'll be coming to talk about—about something."

"Never, my bairn!" exclaimed the woman, clenching her hands in speechless amazement.

"Ay, but it's sae, mother. Father thinks weel o' him now, does he no?"

"But here, Jenniper lass—what—I canna—"

"I'll be just outby." And Jenniper had escaped.

Crozier had lingered about the Howff, not only to contemplate the secluded beauty of the scene. As the distance lessened, he could attend less and less to the pageant around him; calm less and less the fierce throbbing of his heart. Slowly he went up the brae, his eye catching the stare of a daisy, the spangle of a celandine or venturous tormentil, but in an absent way, without his greatly heeding it. Presently Jenniper's geese saw him, and announced the fact in discordant tones to all the wide hills. Crozier could not resist a laugh at this being his first greeting, and the playful notion lightened his thought.

Mrs. Curle stood in the doorway as he came up, and leapt from his horse.

"Ye're travelling the day, Mr. Crozier," said she innocently.

"I am. I hae been through to Newcastle."

"And ye hae yet to get ower to Whaupriggs! Ye'll be tired afore ye're done. But I'm glad to see you. We dinna get many visitors hereaway. Come ben."

Sibbald fastened his horse to the branch of an elder tree that protruded over the wall of the cabbage garden, at one end of the house, and went in.

"David 'ull no be here likely?"

"He's doon to Crawston. Didna ye light on him there?"

"I came along the ridge. I just wanted to hae a look at the old place."

"Ay, ay, ye well might," said the woman in a frankly sympathetic way.

"I wanted a few words with David. We'll be neighbours again some day."

"Ay, ay, I'm sure we hope sae."

"Lord Braiddale is going to sell us the place again."

"Ye dinna say it, Mr. Sibbald!"

The other only smiled at her astonishment.

"But we canna come in before Martinmas twelve month. . . . I didn't want to tell you this, Mrs. Curle. Jenniper ought to have known it first."

"She'll be glad an' a', of course."

Sibbald simply fixed his eyes upon his companion's face calmly, and she returned the look.

"Do you think she will? I wanted to ask her. Is she no here?"

"She's outby."

"May I go to her? . . . Would David object?"

Sibbald's smile alone explained matters, and with a characteristic exclamation the woman dismissed him, she herself sitting down in a chair.

CHAPTER IX.

A FAIRY TALE.

IN the days when she was fancy free, Jenniper had been accounted an imperious and somewhat satirical maiden, who in most situations could give as much as she got. It is possible that the name awarded to her by her grandfather had had a good deal to do with the moulding of that character. Proud of having individual qualities detected and made much of, she was resolved to live up to them. But beneath them were most of the softer qualities that we like to associate with a comely woman. It was only since she had come to have familiar intercourse with young Crozier that she herself was at all aware of her own sensibility. Long before he had in the smallest degree intended—indeed, when his attitude was calculated to have a distinctly opposite effect—his hand had swept the strings of her womanly emotions, and found music to respond.   Utterly hopeless as at that time it seemed, Jenniper was aware that an ideal had stolen into her heart which was not to be removed. Bright enough as this ideal was, it knew nothing of joy ; it lacked all property of human hope.   So that under it Jenniper's life had become extremely changed.

To be standing, picking the grey pealing lichen off the wall, in that April sunshine, with a palpitating consciousness that all this hope had suddenly come, proved a disquieting ordeal, even for the aggressive Jenniper.   The shadows of the little glistening clouds passed over her, and again the sun, and she knew that with any returning ray he also might issue from the house to seek her.   A blackbird, which had found a mate venturous enough to share his moorland soli- tude, whistled his musings from the one sycamore tree that Angryhaugh boasted, and to this Jenniper could attend, for it seemed to sustain the pensive note she required, to utter some of the sober joy that she herself was feeling, if that surface flutter would but have permitted her to feel at all. But suddenly she heard the step, and turning, she found herself calm in a moment.

For Sibbald, too, one glance of the actual Jenniper was sufficient. From it all his tremulous indecision fled, and he came up to her in all the radiance of his most buoyant life. Immediately they were together the need of these logical explanations vanished. Each saw in the opposing eyes all that was wanted, and each instantly understood: a sense of ease and familiarity, a glad deliverance from all restraint, a merging of all self in the glorious counterpart.

" I have been too long, my lassie." But *now* Jenniper was scarcely conscious that he had ever left her.

They turned to the burn-side and walked upwards, talking little until they reached a small crag which jutted from the hill. It was cloven in two at the base, and so formed a natural recess with which the sheep were familiar. Sibbald flung himself on the grass before it, and his companion took a position by his side. From there the whole of the upper dale was before them, and all the hill-tops beyond, also an unbroken view of Bygate opposite. It was in this direction that Crozier inevitably turned his eyes, and Jenniper followed them.

"It was a pity we were turned out of there," said he in a tone of apparent levity, which startled the other. "It's a bonnie place."

Jenniper simply upbraided him by maintaining silence, and keeping her eyes fixed afar.

"Wouldna you hae liked to be mistress there, Jennie?" he added, seizing her reluctant hand, and nipping the flesh above the wrist.

"It's likely I would."

"I could tell you a fairy tale, my bairnie, if you werena so cross. Would you have patience to listen? I heard it in Newcastle the day."

Only with one sharp glance would she condescend to bid him proceed, but he took it, and she turned her eyes again to Bygate.

"Once upon a time there was a castle in the midst of wild hills far away from the haunts of men, where, for many generations, a race of giants lived. From father to son they were a savage people, despising all the rest of the world, and fighting with all who should chance to come in their way. For many a day they flourished and were victorious, but at last clouds arose. The world outside had altered, and although these giants despised the world, arrows from it reached them, and disturbed their savage repose. In gathering fury these they still defied. They hurled rocks and curses at random, broadcast, without quite knowing by whom it was they were assailed. The effect only recoiled upon their own heads. They tore their hair to no purpose. Until one day a pigmy, a mere dwarf even in the common world, came actually to their castle gates and offered them a challenge to mortal combat, on condition that the fight should be upon a field in his world. Had his challenge come alone, it would, perhaps, not have been accepted ; he would have been strung up, and there an end; but this pigmy found the means of secretly introducing into the giants' stronghold a beautiful fairy, who, with the help of an invisible dust which she could throw about her, dazzled the eyes of some of the giants themselves, especially the younger ones, and they saw things which were not what they seemed. This brought a division into the giants' den. Some thought this, some thought that, some blessed, some cursed, until, to settle the difference, they must needs take to blows amongst themselves, and so (as he had, of course, shrewdly foreseen) they fell an easy prey to the victorious pigmy. He drove them from their castle into *his* world, and gave their possessions into strange hands. After they had wriggled and gasped in the new light of their strange surroundings for some time, like trouties just drawn from the burn, they discovered the mistake that they had made, but it was too late. In the quarrels amongst themselves, they had sorely wounded one another. One had lost an arm, another an eye, several even were altogether blind.

" But the burden of all was the same, a pining for their old castle amidst the barren hills, which they could all now see (although they would have died outright rather than have mentioned it to one another) had been lost solely through that magical dust which had been thrown amongst them, But though it had thus overwhelmed them with misfortunes, it had done them good. It had at least shown them that whatever mistakes it had drawn them into, these were not so great as the savage life which it had done so much to destroy. They knew that, if they could but recover their home, their life there would not be as it was before. But it seemed they were to be denied the opportunity of showing it. The dwarf and his fairy, too, had snapped their fingers and disappeared. They seemed to be left utterly in the dark, with nobody even to fight with. Until one day one of the blind giants had a dream ; he thought it was a vision, and that he was awake, and that his eyes were opened ; but no doubt it was a dream, and in this dream another fairy appeared to him, of beauty unspeakable. He was terrified by her splendour, but she touched him, and spoke kindly to him, and made him look up, then she told him that if he would follow her, do all that she bade him, all might yet be well, yes, even to regaining their old home again. It was not destroyed, she said, but a great mountain hid it, to which she would show them the

way, and through which they would have to *dig* their
way.   It might take them years to get through it,
but she promised that if they dug and dug through
it some of them should get to it, and their old loved
castle would appear on the other side with all the
gates open to receive them.   Then the fairy disappeared, but directly afterwards the giant found
that his eyes really had been opened, and staring
about, he saw that there *was* the huge mountain she
had spoken about, and he knew it to be the one, for
the fairy herself was plainly to be seen on the summit
against a brilliant sky.   Fired by this unexpected
announcement, the giant immediately set to work, and
dug and dug with the lightest heart he had known
for a long time.   But soon another wonder was to
befal him.   One day whilst at work, the same old
pigmy that had caused so much of their former misery
appeared to him, although he was so changed that
the giant did not at first recognise him, and said with
tears in his eyes that he had been wandering round
the world seeking rest and never finding it, until a
voice out of the clouds had told him that he never

would find it unless he returned and helped the giants to get back to their home. So he had come. With this he gave the giant a bag of glittering sand, and told him that if he flung this sand as far as he could over the great hill at which he was digging, he would see it immediately disappear, and his old home would be at once before him. Then the pigmy hastily departed, still with tears in his eyes. For some time the giant ceased his work, scarcely able to believe the good news, but as the bag was really in his hand he thought that at least he might try what the dwarf had told him. So he opened the bag and peeped within, but was dazzled by the brightness which came from it, so shutting his eyes he flung the sand with all his might over the hill. When he next looked, instead of that tiny hole which he had dug at the foot of the mountain, he saw his own old home rise in the morning sun before his eyes, and at the door—" here Sibbald paused and looked into the glittering eyes of his companion—"who do you think? That good fairy from the mountain-top. He darted up to her," concluded the narrator, burying one of Jenniper's hands in both of his, " and seized her hand. She tried to escape him, but he held it. . . . And—and she promised never to leave him or the castle—of Bygate ever after."

A silence followed this fantastic display of Sibbald's fancy, until, turning to Jenniper with a radiant visage, he said :

" Darling, it is again all—all our own."

Time did not exist for them, so the pair still were sitting at the foot of the rock when the sun had lowered almost to the rim of the hills bounding the valley. They might have sat there longer, even have been there still, for their theme was a long one, had not the appearance of the shepherd, David Curle, on the opposite bank of the burn, recalled them to their situation. He was returning from his round, his dog behind him, and both stood in speechless astonishment at the spectacle presented. Crozier still held his companion's hand, and continued to hold it. As they both got up, the dog crossed over and sniffed suspiciously at Sibbald's legs, but began to wag his tail. Curle's display was not so immediate, although he too came forward in an uncompromising way. Crozier offered his hand, and it was taken.

"I am glad to see ye, Mr. Crozier."

"I am glad of that," laughed the other. "I was afraid that I ought to have seen you first. You saw that Jenniper had given me her hand."

"I could hardly believe my eyes," said the man frankly. "But I saw it."

"And, I hope, gave your approval."

"I hae never thought that in affairs like yon the parents should hae ower much say in the matter, unless they could see plain that it was for their lassie's harm in this world or the next. I'll no say that I feel it in this case. I hae aye trusted my lass Jenniper's judgment in common things, and I dinna think I need mistrust it in an affair of sic importance. What pleases her will please me, and I'm sure a' bodies speak well o' ye, Mr. Sibbald."

"Thank you for that, father," interposed Jenniper warmly.

"But Jenniper needs a very good man indeed, and that—"

" I winna say that she has no got it."

They all walked down to the house, and it was not until the sun had set that Sibbald took horse.

He had ridden blithely from Angryhaugh to Redesdale once before, but never so blithely as in the spring twilight of that day. . . . The incipient fever had passed, and the man could see something of the genuine depth of his joy now that the surface ripple was in a measure abated. The subdued light in which he was travelling favoured the vein of solemnity that had crept into his joy, and yet made, each moment, more clear the stars which were over all. He took a long time over the journey.

There followed some debate in Sibbald's mind as to the proper handling of his father. He was by no means disposed to defer the fulness of his joy until he could actually enter Bygate, a matter of eighteen months or so, and yet, after what had passed, to propose unconditionally to his father the introduction into their house of a member of the family of Curle, seemed a perilous undertaking. On the other hand, an immediate revelation to the old man of the fact that Bygate was theirs, but that a year and a half must elapse before they could re-enter, seemed little less perilous, if only from the point of view of the intolerable vexation anybody would have to endure from the elder's seething impatience at the delay. It required a day or two to settle, and then at length only with Jenniper's advice.

When she was called upon to decide, her own candid preference was given for an entry into the household of Whaupriggs. She considered that a short apprenticeship there would the better prepare her for the larger responsibilities of the old home—for she was of course ignorant of so much that it was impossible for Sibbald to divulge to her. Of the infinite complexities of his father's irritability he could say nothing, and as he was anxious to direct her advice into the desired channel, he naturally put that irritability upon its simplest basis. On those lines, however, the resolve was made, with a little necessary intermixture from Sibbald as he rode homeward.

The needed interview with his father was not

long delayed. A peculiarly favourable opportunity occurred the same evening, when the old man had come from his den into the general room upon hearing his son's arrival. He had the local newspaper in his hand, and was in a mood for professional conversation.

" Do you see the Barnside sale is fixed for the forst o' May ? " said he, shuffling along over the stones to the fireside, and skilfully lowering himself into the chair always kept there in readiness for him.

" Ay; so I hard the day."

Sibbald was bilingual, and upon common occasions always adopted the vernacular with his father, knowing his preference.

" They'll hae a grand lot yonder."

" A-ha."

Then followed a short silence, during which the old man crumpled the newspaper in his hand, with his eyes fixed upon the fire, and Sibbald got settled at the table for his meal.

" And what arc ye gaun to buy, man ? "

" I hardly ken, daur say. I hae no seen the list."

Strange subdued noises issued from the grizzled

beard, strongly suggesting considerable impatience, if not disgust.

" What do you think ? "

" Ou, I dinna ken. Ye canna gan wrang wi' Barnside. They hae thirty score o' three pairts ewes wi' their lambs . . . or a few score o' the half-bred ewe hoggs, daur say; they're forst cross off Loanend, ye ken."

" But do ye think I'll no get ower mony for sicna place ? "

The old man snorted again ominously.

" We maunna be ower-stocked. It's no just like the old braes. If I had them to stock—as we shall, before sae varry long—but Corsbie has 'em till Martinmas twelve month. My certie, but I'm sorry to miss the Barnside flocks for that—"

" Ye maunna miss 'em," roared his father in a tone of fury; for although Sibbald had uttered his remarks quickly, as though to himself, they had had the intended effect upon the other, but also more. Even Sibbald did not fully recognise the uncertain state of the old man's mind. The hint given had, as a matter of fact, perplexed as much as angered him. The sudden intrusion of an emotional subject into a conversation so purely practical was more than his brain could stand. He got muddled between the two, and after a brief interval of angry, incoherent ejaculations, he got up and shuffled out of the room.

This result was not altogether contrary to Sibbald's expectations, not at all contrary to his hopes. So he finished his meal with satisfaction, and went about the closing affairs of the farm. When he came in again a short time later, to his surprise he found his father re-established in the chair which he had so recently abandoned, and looking, for such a decided character, irresolute and shy. He was scowling with all the vehemence of most expressive eyes and forehead wrinkles, but behind it lurked what to his son seemed nothing short of timidity. No direct glance was given to Sibbald as he came in, but when his back was turned a furtive one would be thrown upon him. When the woman went out of the room, the nature of the glance suddenly altered, and the old man betrayed an unmistakable anxiety to speak.

But she returned, and again he was looking here and there with an increased air of bewilderment.

At length he got up from his chair, and walked to the back door. Sibbald looked after him, astonished at the movement. As the old man stepped out into the darkness of the yard, his son escaped out by another door, to keep a watch upon his movements. It was a clear night, but dark. No moon, but an unclouded expanse of stars, shone over them. From his concealment Sibbald saw and heard his father shuffling about the place on his sticks, and trying the doors. Sibbald himself had just locked them all for the night. At every disappointment there was audible muttering. Ultimately, faintly illumined by the stars, the young man could distinguish the white head raised upwards as though trying to discern either some distant stars, or the contour of the dark hills. Such erratic conduct made Sibbald bold. It differed from all old Crozier's methods, and alarmed his son. Skirting the place quickly, he re-entered the yard by a gate, which he let fall to with a loud clang behind him. This made the dog bark, and come out through the open back door. Sibbald called to it by name, and quieted it. In crossing to him, it passed by the old man, and sniffed at him.

" Is that you, father ? "

There was no answer, but coming close up to the figure, Sibbald found the old man in a state of tremulous agitation, so much so that he condescended to lean his weight upon his son's shoulder.

" I canna mak' it oot, Sib," began the elder in an altogether unexpected tone, one suggesting weakness and impotent perplexity, not rage. " Ye'll think it tarr'ble strange, but I canna mak' it oot, ye ken. Will ye juist tell me whether this *is* the steading o' Bygate, or whether it's *no ?* "

" This is no Bygate," replied the youth as innocently as might be. " This is Whaupriggs, ye ken, where we hae to bide a bit until we can get Corsbie oot o' Bygate. His lease is no up till Martinmas twelve months."

" But I hae gien nae lease o' Bygate, no likely."

" No, but dinna ye mind that thae twa deils, Felton

and David Curle, robbit us of it? It has been the death of 'em; baith on 'em are dead as saut herrings; but no afore they gathered lawful gear, and came to a mind o' their villainy. They hae bought ye Bygate back again, and Felton, that was Brett, ye ken, has just paid a' his debts, every penny on 'em, and your twa thousand pounds an' a'."

Sibbald hurried on, not knowing how much was heard or heeded, aware only of the tremulous agitation of the figure against him.

" They are juist making out the writings to convey a' the property back to you yoursel'."

. " I—I canna mak' it oot."

The old man allowed himself to be led back to the house. Sibbald thought it best to abandon the topic for that night, and throughout the whole of it kept an eye upon his father's room.

For two or three days old Crozier was ill, at least, he was quite bereft of that degree of mental calm he had before attained. There seemed no active ailment beyond this, and the doctor promised that he should soon rally.

Going one morning in to him, Sibbald saw the change had come. Once more the offensive forces had triumphed, and the old features bore a distinctly aggressive air. The young man consequently weighed his words.

" I'm gaun to buy a few score o' the ewes and the half-bred gimmers at Barnside," he began, but his father's eyes flashed upon him in scorn.

" Ye hae no come here to ta'k aboot ewes and gimmers," exclaimed he. " Just gie us the meat o' the maitter."

Still Sibbald affected not to understand him, and was trying once more to maintain his uncompromising subject.

" What's gannin on in yon affair ? " interrupted the elder in a still more violent tone. " Did ye tell me on't, or did ye no ? I winna believe that it's juist a' a dwaum." His eyes were riveted with tragic intensity upon the youth in speaking, and Sibbald could not but see that dissimulation now was the more dangerous method.

' Yes, I spoke on't. They are making out the

writings to convey the whole of your property back to you."

"Then I winna hae't. No an acre, no a whin buss, no a heather shank o' Bygate wull I hae again, sae ye may tell 'em sae. It's no mine I tell ye, and I winna hae't."

Sibbald stood calm, and regarded the old man with a firm gaze. He had occasionally won by such means, and never such need of trying it as now. The look of the other undoubtedly gave way.

"But ye were reft of it by fools and villains," he remarked with warmth enough, but quite free from excitement. "And surely an honest man is entitled to his ain again when they get their deserts."

"It's no mine, and I'll no hae a stick on't," re-asserted the other in a passion.

Attempted persuasion only incensed the old man more, so had to be abandoned.

"But ye'll come and live there again when we get in?" asked Sibbald.

"No, I winna—but—but—I'll gan to die there. I'm deen I tell ye. What hae I to dee wi' property,

wi' writings and the like o' that? I'm deen—clean
deen entirely a'thegither. I'll die there, for I dinna
believe I'll ever get aff frae anywhere else."

Sibbald paused for an instant in the face of this,
and then gave in.

"You mean, then, that I maun hae it a' conveyed
to mysel'?"

"Juist! . . . What else would ye dea? Hae ye
no got a braw life afore ye?"

Beyond this the young man found it impossible
to go, and upon these terms the compromise was
ultimately made.

Despite the initial difficulties, it required but a
short time to reveal the real effect of this change of
prospect upon old Crozier. Gradually, but surely,
his excessive irritability regained on him, and with
it a degree of offensive prowess which had been
lacking for a long time. This indicated the increase of intellectual vigour within him. Now it
could take scarcely any other form, for his old, long-
sustaining vein of humour was utterly drained. He
had recovered enough to be in time for the Barnside

sale, and so despotic was he, and so great the confidence of Sibbald in his professional judgment, that
the latter not only strained his immediate resources,
but even anticipated the prospective ones, to satisfy
the old man's liberal demands upon the famed Barnside flock. All sorts of complex arrangements in
consequence had Sibbald to make for the boarding
out of his excess stock at strange farms, and it began rapidly to be bruited that, canny fellow as he
was, young Crozier was beginning to put his head
just a bit ower forrard, and the inevitable reverse
began accordingly to be foreseen.

This, however, had again to be altered when the
explanation of it all was at length known. The news
entrusted as no secret to the Curle family had soon
sped from end to end of the native dale, and from
there the whaups and the plovers speedily carried it
to the banks of the Rede water. So, instead of
being on the decline, it was whispered that the
young Scholar's prospects were very distinctly in
the ascendant, and an access of popular consideration
and esteem was consequently from that moment his.

This was increased by the Scholar's genial method of taking his good fortune. Lord of Bygate though he was, there was no alteration in the details of his social life. He still busied himself with the concerns of his neighbours, and with increased power at his disposal, those neighbours became largely multiplied.

In one only respect had Sibbald's plans not been successful. After that consultation with Jenniper, it had been his intention to use the restoration of Bygate as a direct introduction of his father to a more personal project still. The result of his first disclosure had precluded his going on to this. Until now they had come to the hay-time, and still the next step had not been taken.

Once or twice in his life before, when he had found difficulty in untying, Sibbald had taken the approved method of cutting, a knot. To this course in a third case he was very rapidly tending. It appeared to him that if he simply claimed Jenniper, wedded her, and brought her home without any preliminary announcement to his father at all, the affair might be simplified. Let the old man simply encounter the girl personally about the premises, and gain his first impression from that very palpable fact, rather than from the mere sound of her somewhat invidious name. Jenniper herself was rather averse from such a perilous method, but Sibbald was urgent and his persuasion was able to prevail.

CHAPTER X.

"The gold is thine ; the land is mine ;
And now I'm again the lord of Linne."

ONE genial September morning Sibbald was in his
gig on the road over the hills from Redesdale
into the Braid valley, a road which in the past few
months he had come to know pretty intimately. He
allowed his horse to go leisurely, and the driver
looked over the fair prospect in a complaisant frame
of mind. It was about noon when he drew up before
the door of Angryhaugh, and immediately he did so
a figure issued from the doorway to greet him.

It was a radiant figure, which the sun took still
further pains to illumine, and might have seemed to
find peculiar satisfaction in doing so. A young
woman it was in the fulness of maidenly beauty, to
the development of which his beams had already in
no small degree contributed, and who now frankly

invoked his aid in the appropriate celebration of a
bright moment which was to crown her life. Her
head was uncovered, and the rays joined with the
breezes in investing her with a halo which greatly
enhanced the clear spiritual charm of the features
around which it played. The dark brown tresses
left the forehead unclouded, and were gathered simply
into a loose knot behind. The strong, graceful form
which sustained these index features was clad in a
simple frock mingled of brown and green, suitably
suggesting the gracefulness it shielded, and as Sibbald
stepped down beside it he merely placed a hand on
one of the shoulders by way of caress and tender
approbation of the simple taste displayed.

"Heaven itself is kind to you, my ain lassie," said
he, in an undertone, and her colour deepened as she
responded to his eyes.

David Curle came out, arrayed in his Sabbath
"cleeding," and insisted upon himself taking the
horse from the vehicle and leading it round to shelter.
When he returned, Sibbald presented him with a
white chrysanthemum, and begged that he should

wear it " for yance." The plain shepherd shook his head and smiled grimly.

" I'm no ower used to the like o' that, Mr. Sibbald," said he, " but I'll aye keep it in the Book, ye ken, in memory of a gude day."

Then he turned with it in his hand into the house. Sibbald laughed good-humouredly.

" I wondered what he would do with it," he said to his silent companion. " You'll no be so squeamish anyway." And he proceeded to adjust, without re-sistance, a single white rose in the bosom of Jenniper's dress. When he had done it he gave her just one light kiss. Then they also went into the house.

It appeared that this plain Braiddale family did not attend to all the proprieties. It had been ar-ranged amongst them that the bridegroom should himself accompany his bridal party to the meeting-house at Crawston, and that the distance between Angryhaugh and the village should be traversed on foot. After, therefore, Sibbald had been pressed to take refreshment in vain, the shepherd expressed his wish to engage in prayer before they should set off on their weighty errand. There they all accordingly knelt, the brilliant sun stepping some distance over the threshold to join them, enveloped in the silence of the eternal hills, whilst the devout father briefly committed the doings of that day into the hands of a higher power, commending to its merciful guidance "thy two children who are this day to begin their earthly pilgrimage together," praying that the journey so begun might prove but a first step to a more righteous and an everlasting kingdom, and that the service in which they were so soon to be engaged might be the means of saving grace to all.

Mrs. Curle had not the scruples of her husband, for the flowers which Crozier had brought her she consented to carry in her hand. In descending the hill, Jenniper and her father went first; the mother and Sibbald followed a short way after. On the opposite slope shone Bygate and its braes in the full brilliance of the noonday sun, and more than one pair of eyes travelled occasionally in that direction. Of audible speech there was scarcely any.

The Presbyterian church had been gaily decorated

by Jenniper's friends and associates at Crawston, nor did these fail to muster in force to testify to their curiosity, or, let us say, sympathetic interest, in the event which their previous efforts were to help to celebrate. Neither bridegroom nor bride was exactly common property of the dale, although, of course, the strongest interest centred in the problematical Scholar of Bygate. Much speculation was indulged as to the prospects of such a union, and opinions were divided. It was taken for granted that the Scholar had heretofore been sufficiently known, therefore his reputed change was a source of congratulation. It was obvious, however, that peace and good-will by a very large measure prevailed.

About an hour later the same simple procession was on its way to Angryhaugh again, the only difference being that the four walked abreast instead of in pairs. Husband and wife formed the centre, flanked by the father and mother of the bride. Jenniper had intended that there should have been five, and the failure of this intention was the only source of dissatisfaction in her mind. On arriving at the church

Jenniper had for an instant been unceremoniously seized at the entrance.

" He's bonnie, my lass ; he's awful bonnie," was whispered in her ear.

" It's too bad o' you, Maggie," was the hurried reply. " We looked out for you as we came down. Will you promise to be here as we come out ? I winna be right married—"

" Ou, ay, hinny," but Maggie had gone, and Jenniper was not to set eyes on her again that day.

By Sibbald's own requirement, he and his bride did not set off on their homeward drive until five o'clock. It was his intention to cross the hills in the evening light, and reach Whaupriggs in the gloaming. When, accordingly, the last ridge was reached, from which the wide vale of the Rede became visible, the sun had already passed below the wild hills at the head of the valley, and shadows were creeping into the bottom of the recesses. Some strips of dark purple cloud lay motionless in the afterglow over the mountains, and a clear evening star appeared, whilst all around the landscape was wrapt in the profoundest slumber.

The hearts of both beat high as they descended into the gathering obscurity before them, and such little conversation as they had sustained on the journey now altogether ceased. As they passed a wood by the roadside, a cock-pheasant piped, but the abrupt and resonant note died away, and no other sound assailed them.

Crozier exercised some precaution in entering his premises, for he wished to avoid any interview with his father that night. Latterly the old man had evinced less and less inclination for intercourse, and, as a rule, never issued from his room after tea-time. It was upon this that his son had built; nevertheless, he went with a stealthy cautiousness to the parlour to see that his instructions had been carried out. To his supremest consternation, as he half stepped through the doorway, the first object that caught his eye was the old familiar figure seated in a chair, and illuminated only by the light from the fire. Checking himself from going farther, Sibbald collided with Jenniper, who was immediately behind, and there was a pause. Then a voice came from within.

"Come away here! If ye'll no invite me to the wedding, ony way I'll come in for the feast."

So immediately giving in to the situation, Sibbald laughed aloud, and called out to the kitchen for the lamp. Taking Jenniper's hand, he led her into the room and forward to the hearth-rug.

Old Crozier did not so much as look up to her, but continued grumbling from his chair.

"Ye're a braw callant to be married, and ye canna prepare a feast. My sartie! I dinna ken what things are coming tee. I wouldna insult a lass by bringing her heame to ditch water and a bit o' bread. It was no the way in my day, I can tell ye. But the breed's dean, clean dean, entirely a'thegither."

As he said this, the maid carried in the lamp, and Sibbald could see better to what the elder was referring. In place of the preparation which he had commanded, the full expanse of the old Bygate table was spread with the largest of the family napery, and upon it was exposed all, in the way of plate, that the family possessed. Crozier or no Crozier, it was but too plain that the energy of the old man had reasserted itself for the proper celebration of this occasion. A glance at the sideboard revealed a regiment of bottles of a tall and stately kind, and various approved meats in addition to what were on the table. Sibbald was amazed. Such a feast must have taken days to prepare—days during which he imagined he was conducting a strictly secret policy. He simply stood aside speechless in his defeat.

" Now, let's hae a look at ye," said the elder, sitting well back in his chair, and signing to Jenniper to appear before him.

This she did with a frank and composed air, standing without misgiving, so that the lamplight fell full upon her, and seasoning her heightened colour with something of a smile. Old Crozier stared, and stared again. Sibbald also looked from the background, where he was standing, and smiled. At last the old man lowered his eyes and made strange noises.

" I didna ken there was sicna lass i' the valley of the Braid onyway," was, however, all his remark.

Seeing that there was no escape, Sibbald gave in,

and conducted the feast in as much of the spirit demanded by his father as he could possibly command.

For a whole hour did the old man sustain this unexpected outburst of his former spirit, then abruptly
and unceremoniously withdrew. Despite his own
genuine glow of contentment, there soon became
something ghastly to the young man's imagination in
the display of unnatural mirth which his father
afforded. Once, for an instant, the elder had even
fancied that there was a whole throng around him,
and had sent a shaft of broad facetiousness across the
table at one of these imaginary shades. But with a
stealthy glance of astonishment at his son, he had
quickly recollected himself. It was not long after this
that he had withdrawn. To the youth, all aglow
with a fervent and exalted fancy, the incident came
as an only cloud on the events of the day. To him
it was as though a sombre figure had suddenly
stepped into the sacred precincts of his joy, and
extinguished, by its sinister presence, the flow of
mirth. When his father had gone, he felt a wave of
dejection sweep over him, and he did not immediately

speak. Jenniper, who took it all more lightly, observed his mood, and, rising, went over to his side.

" Dinna fash yoursel', my laddie," said she, coiling an arm around his neck. " We'll take good care o' him, poor man."

" Ay, ay, that you will, my bonnie one. But I could never ha' thought of this. Come and let us get our breath again."

Sibbald rose up, and, covering her head and shoulders with a woollen shawl, took her from the room, and out into the night air.

It was still dark and starry overhead, but as they went through the farm-yard gate on to the sloping pasture beyond, looking eastward they beheld a light spreading upwards over the obscure sky, and presently a clear golden rim of the great harvest moon peeped over the mountain tops. Slowly it emerged as they walked upwards, until the whole disc stared solemnly at them from the gloom.

Under the wide and profound influence of the night Sibbald soon found his spirit revive. By no means to a level of jocularity, but at least to the calm, unclouded heights which he had of late inhabited. The world had never presented itself to him as a field for jocularity, nor was it now likely that it ever would. Nevertheless, he had never been afflicted with constitutional gloom. His temperament appeared to share the character of the elements upon which it had been so largely reared. Merry or sad, there was habitually a sober mien preserved, with a suggestion of reflective balance over all. If the wind had for a moment whistled in petulance, or even howled in fury, it had by its own energy rent the clouds and restored the sun or the stars to their proper courses.

"Have you brought your pistol, Jennifer?" Sibbald suddenly asked, as the moon was gathering power.

She laughed at him, but refused to answer.

When at last the earth was getting lighter, and black shadows appeared before them, they were on their way to the house.

For two or three days old Crozier kept resolutely to his room. Upon his son's visits to him he found him nothing different, except that he was grim, uncommunicative, and wanted to be left alone. One morning when Jenniper was active at her work, she started at the sound of the old man's door. It had been opened, and the shuffling steps came on. He entered the kitchen, and the young woman who happened to be there alone, looked up to greet him, but he kept his eyes resolutely turned away. He walked over to his chair and sat down. Then he watched the figure at its employment, but Jenniper did not again seek his glance.

"What are ye deeing here?" presently came to her in a tone of real or simulated surprise.

"I hae come to look after you," was the unhesitating response, and again there was a momentary pause.

"I dinna want ye to look after me."

"Varry likely, but I ken better than you. Twathree days will alter your opinion."

There was calm assurance in Jenniper's announcement, and a play of delicate humour in her tone. To his frowns and ejaculations she did not look up, nor respond. She went on with her work as if in unconcern.

The old man, on the other hand, scarcely removed his eyes from her. He frowned and resented her behaviour, but he examined her features intently none the less. After that he got up and walked to the doorway. In it he turned, and after one more display of that eager scrutiny, he said, " Well, ye'se a tarr'ble bonnie lass, ony way." Thereupon he went out.

Every morning for a week he paid a similar brief visit to the kitchen when he knew that Jenniper alone was there. Their interchange of words became no more abundant, nor was there any alteration in its tone, but the young housewife soon divined that she was acceptable to the old critic, and so a great source of anxiety was removed. She soon ventured upon trifling exercises of authority with impunity, and she knew that her triumph was supreme. In a very short time that chair in the kitchen became the habitual position of the old man, from which he watched the movements of his indefatigable daughter. But they hardly ever spoke.

Having fallen into these more placid paths, life at

Whaupriggs proceeded calmly for a whole year, but as the days of the following autumn crept on, there was an increasing spirit of unrest amongst the household, to which nobody would refer, but of which all were equally conscious. The irritability of old Crozier had again revived, and although he did not abandon his situation at the chimney corner, there were occasions when Sibbald absented himself from home upon which his behaviour, even to Jenniper, became intolerable. The fact was that the old man was perfectly well aware of what these absences portended, and he probably railed at all established things, because of his own incapacity for taking a part in the preparations they implied. The day at length came when even Jenniper was to spend the day away, and upon some utterly false excuse or explanation being offered him, the reprobate raised his stick in fury against her, and bade her tell him nae lies.

It was in the course of that day's occupation at Bygate that Sibbald and his wife resolved to make one more experiment with the elder, since secrecy from the outset had so miserably failed them. On their return late in the evening, amidst the wind and rain, the old man had withdrawn to his den, and no steps were taken to assail him there. The next morning, however, he reappeared, but his humour was only too visibly written in his features. None the less, Sibbald made the attempt, adopting the semi-tone of authority that had occasionally prevailed.

" I want you to come ower wi' me to Bygate, father, to hae a look round, and see what you would like to hae done there. We'll get in by the twelfth."

Ominous grunts and excessive flashing of the eyes were the only answer, but active violence none. So Sibbald persevered, but not for long.

" Ha'd your tongue, man ! " cried the victim of his well-meant solicitude in a frenzy. " Ye ken weel that the place is neane o' mine. Let them to whom it belangs see what's wanted to be dean. It's gude enough to die in ony way."

The subject was immediately altered, nor was any attempt again made.

During those few days preceding their exodus, not

even Jenniper's tact was capable of soothing the old
man, so he had to be left rigorously alone. In the
meantime, preparations at the other end had actively
proceeded. By amicable arrangement with the
departing tenant, possession of the house had been
obtained a fortnight before the actual quarter day, as
Sibbald wished to do much to the ancestral abode to
worthily celebrate its re-acquisition. This he could
do on a liberal scale, as the excess value of the
unfortunate Felton's estate, after all possible claims,
had amounted to between four or five thousand
pounds. One room, however, remained intact, and
that was her father's parlour. That was to be
rehabilitated for the old man's use as far as possible,
exactly to its former state.

On the eleventh of November, a brilliant day, with
a high west wind and glistening clouds, after previous
heavy rains, Sibbald crossed twice from Whaupriggs
over to the Braid water. First in the morning with
his wife, in advance of a load of furniture : secondly,
in the afternoon, with a dejected, shattered old man,
who looked furtively about him all the way and never

spoke one word. Upon the arrival of the latter Jenniper nodded to her husband, and he went away to the stables. The old man stood on the threshold, supported by his two sticks, staring westwards, where the sun was sinking in glory of pearl, amber and amethyst beyond the hills. The young woman had been about to address him, but, seeing his face, checked herself and drew back. All was intensely silent, and the scene, late in the year though it was, was diversified and beautiful. Jenniper heard a robin singing from a gate in the yard, the clear, crisp, blithe, little song ringing far in the stillness. But to it aa'd Crozier was deaf. His bruised, chaotic soul was listening to far other and more tragic voices. At length he turned as though to enter, and Jenniper was immediately beside him. He glanced hurriedly in her face, with timidity rather than rage, but almost a smile succeeded as he held up one hand to lay it on her shoulder. Thus they went in.

By her labour of the day (from Sibbald's instructions), the old parlour presented exactly its old appearance, and the farmer received a shock of surprise as he beheld it. From his glance into the room he looked into the face of Jenniper, and she saw him shaken by an overwhelming paroxysm of emotion.

"Oh, my lass, my lass!" he muttered, and allowed himself to be led to his old chair. There Jenniper left him.

CHAPTER XI.

AT THE HOWFF AGAIN.

MORE years had sped, and spring was again upon the moors,—a brilliant, fitful spring, as best becomes this spoilt darling of the year. Under soft, cloudless skies had the first curlews arrived, only to be silenced a week later by deep snow and a wind from the north-east, brandishing its glittering sabre over the heads of all that had ventured to take a rash step into his territories.

But by the end of April all was for a time placid and genial again. Daisies and celandines peeped forth from the bent at the summons of the skylarks to behold the fleecy cloudlets, which passed now and then between them and the sun. The bog-myrtle, with little opening catkins, gave its spicy fragrance to the breeze, and to the voice of lark and curlew were
255

added those of the travelled and more fastidious
songsters.

Under such conditions Bygate relaxed his grim
old visage into a smile, and the sober fir trees, who so
well sustained his darker humours at the back, did
their utmost to accommodate a funereal rigidity to
these more spirited requirements. There were already enough lambs on the brae to make the sunlight
plaintive with their cries, and all the little sounds of
the farm life spread far in the noonday stillness. On
one morning of particular splendour, Sibbald had
paused on the crest of Yardhope, his boundary line
at the back, to look around. He did still occasionally in these days, for with his later life he had found
a confirmation of his imaginative fervour. For a few
moments he banished from his mind the state of
markets, the prospective washing and shearing of the
sheep, the drilling of the turnip crop, and looked
upon the face of earth and sky as an inspiring
spectacle which claimed a peculiar affinity with something in his own soul. The very lightest breeze
played about him, whispering round the edge of his

cap, bringing and carrying away the buzz of an
adventurous fly, but in no way asserting itself in
opposition to the universal calm. His house he
could not see, for the belt of fir trees interposed. But
little Angryhaugh of vital memories was there in the
crease on the opposite slope, the wide green valley
with its river dancing in the sun, lying between, and
elsewhere the two or three other remote dwellings
that dotted this part of the dale. Gradually the
man's mind travelled to human things; thrust upon
him, perhaps, by way of contrast to this placid scene.
Episodes in his own past life and those of his family
rose before him, and he marvelled. It seemed strange
to him now that in a universe of order such as this,
man alone should be instinctively and inevitably
prone to the construction of a huge edifice of disorder
upon it. A new sound drew his eye, and what he
saw seemed to come by way of direct furtherance of
these thoughts. Just issued from the gate at the
corner of the plantation, where the expanse of gorse
mingled with the heath, was his little boy, shouting
to a rook, and behind him hobbled an old man be-

tween two sticks. His poor old father! This was the scene upon which he had been reared, and from which he could gather no saner message. It was passing strange.

He watched the two go on, the voice of the child still rising to him, as he chased and threw stones at the rabbits; then they dropped into the little hollow amongst the gorse, and Sibbald himself went on.

It was not that old Crozier was in any sense a companion to the child, although on fine days they generally thus roamed about together, either in the farmyard or the ground adjacent. Decrepitude had not in this case brought its mitigating property of childishness. The extremes found nothing whatever in common. The elder was constantly muttering to himself, and apparently engrossed in ceaseless rumination of neither a playful nor merely irresponsible kind. They seldom exchanged a word. The child would inevitably shout at his fellow, shower questions upon him; but if it was not altogether disregarded, it would be testily resented.

" Ha'd away noo! . . . Come by here! . . . Come
in ahint!"

Old catches of word and tone used formerly for
the dogs would be flung out at him without any
regard to their relevance. But the child was familiar
with it by this time, and was neither repelled nor
frightened by what would have put another four-year-
old to terrified flight. His little sister of two was
never permitted by her mother to accompany them.

It was about an hour later that Sibbald got back
to the house for dinner. In a sunny corner of the
yard by the back door, on some straw covered
with a horse-rug, sat a rosy, blue-eyed child with a
couple of dolls, and a hen with her group of chickens
picked at the straw which surrounded her. Sibbald
caught sight of her as he entered, and creeping
stealthily round by the shed, he came behind
her without being detected. From his pocket
he began to throw handfuls of daisies, celandines, and
dog-violets right over her, and then drew into hiding.
The little woman looked up in astonishment about
her, to the door, to the sky, but without success, and

still the flowers came down upon her.   So she philo-
sophically gave it up, and began to collect the scattered blossoms.   Whilst she was doing this the whole
of her couch began to move, and she to be drawn
backwards with it.   Then turning her head, Kitty
saw the culprit.

"Oh, fa-vey, you canny man!" cried she, using a
family pet phrase which she had picked up.   And
Sibbald flung her up to arms' length.   But the little
cheeks flushed, and the child struggled to be free,
crying, "Dinna, dinna," in a very angry voice.

"Kitty, Kitty!" came in admonitory tones from
the doorway, and Jenniper came out.   Whilst mother
and child were getting together the flowers, for the
latter vehemently protested that everyone must be
picked up, the little boy who had been out with his
grandfather came running into the yard in great excitement, and seeing Sibbald, immediately went to
seize his hand.

"Come away, father; come away!" he cried,
tugging his father furiously in the direction he
wished.

" What is it, my man ? "

" I dinna ken ; but come away quick."

" Not now, Ronald," interposed his mother with authority. " Come away to your dinner. You hae been ower long."

Sibbald looked from one to the other in astonishment. The agitation of the child was obvious, and evidently arising from more than self-will.

" And where's your grandfather ? " asked Jenniper.

The child only tugged at his father, and burst into tears. Quick, grave looks were exchanged by husband and wife, and Sibbald, saying he had better go, followed his little boy's leading.

They went out of the yard, and by the plantation, evidently towards the spot where Sibbald had seen the two from the hill-top. He tried another way to pacify the child, and get him to explain what had happened, but without any success. Now that his tears had begun, nothing would stop them. As he tore his father forwards, he wept continuously, only stammering through his trouble, " I dinna ken, I dinna ken," to every form of persuasion. As they passed through the gate, a wave of scent from the blooming gorse met them, and a couple of partridges flew away.

"Are you going to grandfather, laddie?" said Sibbald again, in a coaxing tone, but still there was no reply.

Along the little stony track he went, a track sprinkled with white moorland sand, and which in wet weather was a rivulet of moorland water. Then he left it and turned amongst the knobs of gorse, over the short, fine grass, nibbled to velvet, until he came to a bit of dark crag, by which in summer the foxgloves grew, and behind which was a slight depression in the ground like a fairy hollow. Sibbald then saw what he had expected, and a thrill of deep emotion passed through him.

"Look, father!" said the little fellow excitedly, pointing down below. "I canna—canna wake him. . . . Is he dead like Jockie?"

This referred to a tame squirrel of the child's that had died two days before.

"Yes, Ronald, he's dead."

"But winna he wake again at a'?"

Strangely, the little boy's tears had ceased now, and he looked into his father's face with a wistful expression of wonder which touched Sibbald's heart.

"In heaven he will. Never here again at a'," he replied, falling unconsciously into Ronald's inflection. "We all die when we get old, and, laddie, it's bonnie to die in the open sun like that. . . . Now, run home, darling, and ask mother to send David to me here." And off Ronald ran.

It was a source of infinite consolation to Sibbald to see what a placid object the old man presented— on his little boy's behalf. In the awful circumstances under which the child had been left, and from the singular behaviour he displayed, he had feared for any tragical picture of death, such as might have affected the little fellow's imagination for life. Happily, all was placid as the scene around. At the foot of a small birch tree the figure lay in an easy and composed posture, whilst a yellow hammer sang to him on a branch above. Sibbald went down, and, kneeling by his father's side, took his hand to assure himself the pulse was still, then he placed his face

close to the gnarled old features, calmer than they
had been for half a century, but there was neither
pulse nor breath.

Sitting on the grass beside the silent figure, and
musing principally to the soft dirge of a cushat from
the plantation at hand, Sibbald awaited the coming
of the hind. When the man came they carried their
burden to the house, and all was as before.

The death of "aa'd Crozier," as Sibbald's father had
been known for years, excited considerable interest,
if not deep mourning, throughout the countryside in
which he had been a familiar object for so long.
When, therefore, a few days later, he was to be " put
away," as his neighbours termed it, within the sacred
precincts of the Howff, the isolated burial-ground
in the valley below Bygate, there was a considerable
concourse of people. It was not a brilliant day, but
one of those brooding, contemplative days of spring
when the hills lie clear for miles beneath a sombre
sky of grey marble.   There was no wind at all, and
in the solemn silence of the graveside Sibbald heard

from the head of the valley the barking of dogs, and the confused clamour of sheep, and he knew that the shepherd at the Peel was "louping" his flock into the river for their bath preparatory to clipping. The thought of this rather than any more appropriate reflection occupied him through the greater part of the service. Grief at the old man's departure he could not feel, and the merely contemplative aspect of it had already occupied many of his thinking moments, and so had perhaps little left to impart. The rest now to which the apparently restless had attained was proclaimed by everything around, and in that fact alone lay a profound source of consolation. Despite all tragical discoveries and disclaimers, Sibbald saw in that grave the heir of a line of Croziers to whom there was no successor. With the turf which should lie softly upon that fevered frame was closed one other page of the immeasurable human volume, and only with the closing of it did the full expanse of the new page appear to him. It was to this rather than to regrets and commiseration that his face was turned as with Jenniper alone he mounted the brae to the house of his fathers.

"They aye called me the Scholar, Jennie," said he as they went in, "but I dinna think that until to-day I hae ever got *into* the school."

THE END.

Printed by Cowan & Co., Limited, Perth.

www.ingramcontent.com/pod-product-compliance
Lightning Source LLC
Chambersburg PA
CBHW020347030726
47496CB00007B/2039